Henry Kingsley

The Grange Garden

A Romance. Vol. II

Henry Kingsley

The Grange Garden
A Romance. Vol. II

ISBN/EAN: 9783744777124

Printed in Europe, USA, Canada, Australia, Japan

Cover: Foto ©Andreas Hilbeck / pixelio.de

More available books at **www.hansebooks.com**

THE
GRANGE GARDEN

A Romance

BY

HENRY KINGSLEY

AUTHOR OF
'THE HILLYARS AND THE BURTONS' 'NUMBER SEVENTEEN' ETC.

IN THREE VOLUMES—VOL. II.

London
CHATTO AND WINDUS, PICCADILLY
1876

LONDON : PRINTED BY
SPOTTISWOODE AND CO., NEW-STREET SQUARE
AND PARLIAMENT STREET

CONTENTS

OF

THE SECOND VOLUME.

THE GRANGE GARDEN.

CHAPTER I.

ARTHUR DOCTORS STRUAN.

Struan was as well dressed and as charming as ever, and greeted Arthur in the most friendly manner. A handsome breakfast had been prepared for him, to which the three sat down socially.

'And Dr. Cross is not with you, I understand,' said Struan.

'No, he is on the Continent,' said Arthur.

Struan looked up quickly. 'Oh, you are mistaken; I saw him in London this morning.'

Arthur could not help looking rather disturbed, but Struan did not seem to notice it.

'Did you speak to him?' said Arthur.

'Yes; I told him that I had been staying with you for ten days, and that you were kind enough to invite me to renew my visit; that I had accepted your invitation, and was coming.'

George could not help smiling at the sudden destruction of all Arthur's plans for keeping his new friendship secret from Cross.

'It is my opinion,' he said, by way of re-assuring his brother, 'that Cross will turn up to-day, on wheels.'

'Turn up on wheels?' said Arthur. don't see what you mean.'

'I mean that he will come in a carriage,' said George, in a very conciliatory manner. 'I did not mean any harm, Arthur.'

'You mean something or another,' said Arthur, ' or you would not be so civil.'

But George and Struan both laughed at this; and Arthur, who was never very ill-natured, laughed also.

Cross did not come that day, and it was passed very pleasantly. Struan's conversation seemed to elevate both Arthur and George. They did not quarrel at all during the day. Struan talked about Arthur's going into Parliament, and urged it on him. Arthur said that he was such a fool. Struan disagreed with him entirely about that matter, and in short they got on very well. The horses were shown, trotted out, and inspected, but Struan did not buy. After lunch he went over the house with Arthur, looking at many things, some of which Struan was prepared to buy, some of which he was emphatically inclined to leave alone. Still Arthur

saw a very good market, and rather wished
that he could have bought George off at less
than one-third.

In the middle of a long gallery, when
they were both alone, Struan looked at
Arthur very steadily.   Arthur naturally
looked at him in return, and noticed that
Struan was very pale and faint.   Arthur came
to his assistance at once, and good-naturedly
asked what was the matter.

' I am in extreme pain, Mr. Branscombe,'
said Struan ; ' would you give me your arm
to my bedroom ? '

Arthur at once did so.   The fit of pain
was very heavy, but Struan stood it like a
man.   When Arthur got him on to his bed,
Struan got him to go through certain details
which are not necessary to mention here.
They were of a rather difficult nature, such
as a man generally requires a surgeon for.

Arthur was a tolerable surgeon; he bred a large number of horses, most of them sound, and therefore required the presence of a veterinary surgeon but seldom. But the vet.'s bills were long, and as the veterinary surgeon had a reputation to keep up, he was not always to be depended on in a case of warranty. Arthur had tried several of them, and they all had the infernal habit of speaking the truth when put on their oaths. That would not do, and so Arthur, from Blaine and Youatt, got up the subject for himself, and saved money, not to say worry. He therefore had a tolerable knowledge of anatomy, and as regards therapeutics or pharmacy, he could have treated his own brother for the farcy or spavin with eminent success; but then his brother George never had those diseases, nor indeed any others, being a peculiarly virtuous and healthy living young man.

He however made an excellent diagnosis
of Struan's malady. 'You have,' he said, a
large sebaceous tumour pressing on that
artery. If you were a horse of mine, I
should put the knife to it; I will do it for
you if you like; two of my grooms could
hold you down easily, and there is not the
least danger, because the thing has formed
a callus, and that is what *I* never saw
before. Say the word, and it is out in ten
minutes.'

Struan, looking steadily at Arthur,
laughed at this new form of hospitality, and
declined. He said that the trouble caused
to him by it was merely neuralgic, and that
he would rather not be operated upon, but
would get up.

But Arthur was discontented. 'It would
be easier to me than bleeding a horse on the
palate for megrims,' he said. 'I shifted it

for you very well; however, if you like to
wait until Cross comes, as I suppose he
will——'

'Mr. Branscombe,' said Struan, 'would
you do me the favour not to mention this
little affair to Dr. Cross? Say simply that I
was taken ill; do not say how.'

'I will do as you ask me,' said Arthur,
'but I think you are foolish. Cross is a first-
rate man, and to please me he would practise
as surgeon.'

'I would rather that Dr. Cross knew nothing of it,' said Struan.

'Well, then, he shall not,' said Arthur,
still sitting on the bed. 'I want to say
another thing. Don't you think so bad of
my brother George as he looks. He is a
selfish, godless fellow, like myself; but if
you pay him he will behave like a gentleman. But then it takes such a pile of

money to pay him, and I like my money, so we quarrel. And George does not do any harm with his money, like some people; he only gambles, which is inconvenient to me because I have to pay when he loses: and then he wins sometimes. I wish you would try to like George; he is not a bad fellow at all.'

Struan rose up in his bed and looked at Arthur Branscombe more steadily than ever. He looked as if he was going to say a great deal; he only said,

'Arthur Branscombe, if we were much together I should like you; it is brave of you to plead for your scoundrel of a brother, who you know in your inmost heart would sell his soul for a thousand pounds.'

'He would not do that,' said Arthur. 'He says that he has no soul, and that there is no devil. It stands to reason that he could not offer to sell a thing he did not possess to a person who did not exist.'

This flight of theology left Struan leagues behind. He did not say that he saw the same thing done on the Stock Exchange every day; and it did not occur to him until afterwards, when the point of the remark was not appropriate. He merely said,

'I will not say anything more about your brother. You have treated me with the very greatest kindness, and I thank you.'

Arthur made one of his long pauses, then he said,

'You do not conceive that I have been kind to you on mercenary grounds?'

'I know that you have not, Arthur,' said Struan; and so they parted.

Struan was perfectly well by dinner-time, only he walked a little lame. He sat rather long over the wine, though he did not drink much. He had coffee, and at eleven o'clock retired to his bedroom.

At twelve George came to his bedroom. They went into the flower garden and smoked there; then they came back and parted at Struan's door. It was noticeable that they did not in any way disturb the household by so doing.

'And that is the way Cross comes and goes,' said Struan, as he blew his candle out. 'He must be an ass, or he would have poisoned George for showing him the secret, and kept it to himself.'

CHAPTER II.

'MADELEINE,' said Lady Alice one day, 'I wish you had my strength of character.'

'I fancy that I have, Alice,' said Lady Madeleine, 'and a little to spare.'

'You want resolution,' said Lady Alice.

'I was not aware of it,' said Lady Madeleine. 'I am resolute enough; you surely know that.'

'Yes, possibly when you are roused you are resolute for a time, but you are apt to change sides.'

'I can examine evidence, and alter my

opinion when fresh evidence is brought before me.'

'That is a fault,' said Lady Alice. 'When I once make up my mind, I never change it.'

'That is the only weakness in your character, Alice. How can you possibly be so silly? Science, not to mention the Christian religion, would be impossible if the world was ruled by such a theory. You mean obstinacy, a vice, when you talk of resolution, a virtue.'

'Well, then,' said Lady Alice, laughing, 'I'll not have you call me vicious, and so I'll alter me mind to plase ye, though it's but seldom me fawther's daughter does that same.'

'I wish you would not talk Irish, Alice,' said Lady Madeleine, allowing the cloud which had for an instant obscured her mild temper to pass away, but unwilling to show it too quickly. 'And you should not accuse me of want of resource.'

'I never did.'

'You implied it. I am a person of singular firmness of purpose. I remember when I was a mere child that my father said in my presence if Mr. Wilberforce carried a certain resolution the country would be in a state of anarchy, in six months, to which the state of things in France would be nothing; and all his friends agreed with him. I confused the word resolution with revolution, and at once, with the examples of the French nobility before me, buried all my toys in the garden, except one doll, who, as I had determined, was worthy to share my exile or my fate. I judged from the expression of her face that she was capable of great things. She was exactly like your old friend Lady Ballyskerry. Her I did up in a brown paper parcel. Now, I think that showed resource in a child.'

'So you followed the example of Madame Dubarry, did you ? ' said the incorrigible Lady Alice. ' Well, my dear, there was one thing you never resembled her in.'

' And what was that ? ' said the innocent Lady Madeleine.

' Her good looks.'

' I am not so sure,' replied Lady Madeleine, now in high good humour. ' You remember that dreadful old Mrs. Toreker. Well, when I first came out I was a most distinguished failure, and she said to me at Almack's, before everybody, " Lady Madeleine Howard ! oh my dear, I remember you a child, and do you know you were really rather nice-looking then." And then she looked round as if she was prepared for incredulity, if not contradiction.'

'What did you say?'

'I was too frightened to say anything.'

'I,' said Lady Alice, 'should have told her that I did not believe it, for the simple reason that she said it, and no other. If that had not been enough for her, I should have said that I at all events had not got the *sobriquet* of Mrs. Eighteenpence, as she had, in consequence of having one of her eyes twice as big as another.'

'I have no doubt that you would have done so,' said Lady Madeleine. And indeed she was right : one of the reasons which led to the non-success of Lady Alice in the great world was that her powers of sarcasm habitually outran her discretion.

'And so,' said Lady Madeleine, ' you goodnatured and best of souls, you agree to have Lionel's wife here for a short time, in order that we may get her to talk to us, and we with our profound arts of dissimulation may worm out the secrets of her inmost heart.'

'Exactly,' said Lady Alice. 'And if things go wrong, remember that I protested against it, and only yielded to your violence.'

'We understand that.'

'Poor thing,' said Lady Alice; 'she will find it dull here after that dissipated convent. No giddy whirl of ceaseless society among the best-bred girls in five empires; no extremely good-looking middle-aged bishops, or even cardinals, to converse with; no easy, habitual, and confidential society with one of the least vulgar of all the royal ladies in Europe; nothing but two singularly ugly and dull old women to take the place of all this. She will wish herself back pretty soon.'

'She had nowhere else to go at first,'

said Lady Madeleine. 'And you and I do not want to stop short in a work which we began with our Lionel.'

'Best of women, no. But, seriously, will she not be dull here?'

'She was dull there, or she would not have come away,' said Lady Madeleine. 'She will be dull here or anywhere, restless here or anywhere, until that great aching void in her heart is filled. That is my opinion. She has a want, my beloved Alice, which we have never known. Neither of us has ever loved a man, and lost him!'

The room was nearly dark when Lady Madeleine said this, and there was silence for a time; then Lady Madeleine felt the strong hand of Lady Alice holding her delicate weaker fingers, and from that simple touch she knew a secret which she had never guessed during all the years they had lived together: the rough Lady Alice had loved.

The room grew dark by degrees, yet still they said nothing save what the clasped hands could say to one another of confidence and sympathy. Lady Madeleine had never thought of this before, and at last, breaking the long silence, she said, 'Alice, who was he?'

'Your brother Algernon.'

And a great light broke upon the eyes of Lady Madeleine.

CHAPTER III.

Mrs. Lionel Branscombe, in approaching the world, after her long seclusion, got more and more frightened as she went on. Whether that was part of Father Wilson's plan as regarded her, we cannot say,— perhaps he did not exactly know himself, but, like many great generals, Napoleon included, put down the mistakes of his enemies as x, or an unknown quantity in his calculations.

x and y, regarded mathematically, are abominably unruly letters in the hands of

c 2

inexperienced calculators—they may turn
out to be anything, from an Austerlitz to
a Waterloo; from a Solferino to a Sedan,
from a Bullrun to a Gettysburg; or, again,
may be found to represent the failure in
a scholarship and the mean life of a teacher,
or a fellowship and a bishopric. Father
Wilson did not consider these things, or
care much about them. As regarded Mrs.
Lionel, it was not worth his while to do so;
she was rather unimportant. Still he had
taken her husband's and her matter in
hand, and was interested in it: he would,
had he been a secular man, have betted
that Mrs. Lionel would be found back at the
convent in a year. Probably the chances
went that way very strongly at one time.

She was unused to the noise and confusion of travelling alone, and her nervous-
ness was so great that she attracted attention.

She hid herself in trepidation in the darkest corners of the waiting rooms, and could not be made to understand that she had to take two tickets, one for herself, another for her luggage. She fled from the ticket offices, leaving her change behind her, and got shouted after in crowds to her unutterable horror : she was brought back through the staring unmannerly rudeness of the Belgian people, and laughed at for her folly, by a population rude because utterly cowardly. At last she made the grand *fiasco* of taking the wrong train, and getting herself carried into France : had she continued to travel in Belgium, she would probably have gone back.

Landed early in the morning at the Lion d'Or at Autrin, she at once told the whole story to Madame of the hotel. Mrs. Lionel being handsome, religious, and ex-

tremely well-spoken, when she was not
frightened, Madame at once took her case
up with an energy amounting to ferocity.
Her husband, a very 'straight' voter on
the Bonapartist side, proceeded in an Ame-
ricain to the frontier, two miles off. Having shaken his ten fingers in front of the
Belgian *douanier's* nose, until they looked
like twenty ; having demanded of that official
how long he conceived that His Imperial
Majesty would wait before annexing Belgium ;
having paid what was demanded and counted
the change in the most offensive manner,
he returned in triumph with Mrs. Lionel's
boxes, and from that moment became the
gentle kindly Frenchman whom we know
so well, and whom, in spite of all his errors,
we love so well.

Fancy eliminating France ! Shall we see
the sun of good humour and pleasantness

banished from the terrestrial heavens? Accursed be he who dreams of it! The unutterable and atrocious wrongs which this English Catholic lady had suffered from the hands of the Belgian boors was very much talked of in the hotel that morning. It was understood that she had been induced to come to the *table d'hôte,*—a place had been reserved for her, and she came in before everyone was seated, very nervous, but very handsome. The French women had put flowers all round her plate, and she saw the compliment, but did not know what to do: with a mere instinct she rose and bowed, and several ladies bowed in return.

The French ladies were divided on the question as to whether she was most like Marie Thérèse or Queen Victoria. As these two ladies, possibly the most eminent in modern times, have no resemblance in feature,

it is possible that the French ladies had been
reading history from writers of the calibre
of M. Thiers.   An American lady, of great
personal beauty, claimed to know a lady by
the name of Pollex, living in some innumer-
able street, Fifth Avenue, New York, who
was handsomer than Mrs. Branscombe.   An
old French lady who sat next the American
lady, said that she could well believe it, after
seeing the beauty of Madame (the American
lady).   And so they went on making things
pleasant just as though there were not two
millions of German soldiers over the frontier
ready to make things entirely unpleasant.

Mrs. Branscombe had not been in France
before, and she rested here a few days; for
the gentle French ladies made life very agreeable to her.   If she spoke of the convent,
they said that a well-conducted convent was
a heaven upon earth.   If she spoke of the

rudeness of the Belgians, the Belgians were mere dogs, not to be noticed,—of course they ridiculed a lady like herself. If she spoke of England, the English were not all like Madame in *esprit*, but they were good and brave, though stupid. Madame was unlike her compatriots; she had not pronounced teeth, her clothes were well cut, and the colours were good. Monsieur was not with Madame? Well, those things would occur, even in France; *que voulez-vous?*

But she had set her feet for one place, and she could rest nowhere else. She told the old French lady that she had promised to go to Grange Garden, and she described the *ménage* to her.

'Well,' said the old French lady, 'I should go there. Yes, I would have you go there. Mais Monsieur?' .

'Il est mort.'

' A vous?'

' Mais oui.'

' Hein! hein! Les hommes sont tous comme cela. Always faithless!'

' My Lionel was never that. I fear that villains made mischief between us.'

This was the first time she had ever said so aloud. The French lady administered comfort. ' C'était la même chose avec moi,' she said; and then she told Mrs. Lionel her history, as to one with whom she had much in common in misfortune; though she had never heard a word of Mrs. Lionel's affairs.

The history of the French lady was not an improving one, and Mrs. Lionel felt herself misunderstood, and longed to be back at the convent, where such things were never talked of from one year's end to another. The world seemed cruel and scandalous; she

would have gone back to Waterloo, but the
frontier was between her and it. She must
on to England.

Somehow England was more homely and
less terrifying to her than even France; no
one seemed to take the remotest notice of
her, good or bad; if there was not the never-
ending good-nature of France, there was also
none of the freedom and *empressement* of that
country; there was privacy in every hotel and
in every railway carriage. She had no difficulty in finding her way to London unattended,
and there she was waited on at the Grosvenor
Hotel by an extremely respectable looking
middle-aged woman, who told her that she
had been sent by Lady Madeleine to act as
her lady's maid as long as she thought fit to
retain her services. This was an inestimable
boon, and in her heart she fervently blessed
the thoughtfulness of the kind heart which

had conferred it. The woman was a Roman
Catholic, and took her to church in the
morning, to her great comfort, for she had
been afraid to go by herself in France.

So the journey to Shropshire was made
easy to her, and at Shrewsbury a carriage
was waiting for her with private servants
in rather brilliant liveries. She asked her
new attendant whether it was Lady Madeleine's, and she said, No, it was Mr. Wotherston's, and that he was sheriff that year,
and so the men were wearing their full-dress
liveries in the daytime, according to the old
fashion. 'A great man for old customs was
Mr. Wotherston, though he was a Whig,'
she remarked further.

'He lives here, does he not?'

'When not at his duties in the House,
madam.' A gentleman with eighteen thousand good acres to look after naturally has

to look sharp after them if he wants things
to go well.

'Is he much changed?' asked Mrs.
Lionel simply.

'Since when, madam?' said Jeffkins, with
a curious look.

'I mean is he married?' said Mrs. Lionel,
correcting herself.

'No, madam. The squire is a bachelor.'

'Does he go often to the Grange?'

'Yes, madam, most days.'

Mrs. Lionel talked no more until the
hospitable doors of the Grange were opened
to her, which she entered with most singular
trepidation. She was shown into the drawing-room by a *footman* (the italics are ours),
where our two ladies awaited her, not in
state by any means, but with every symptom
of violent gardening about them.

'Here she is,' said Lady Alice in a loud

voice. ' She has grown very fat ; but in my opinion she is handsomer than she was before. They evidently don't starve people in those precious old convents of yours, Madeleine. My dear love, you are so very welcome ; come and have some wine and biscuits. *I* made the biscuits ; who made the wine I don't know ; some Portugee papist, I doubt ; but even *they* can't spoil the blessings of a Protestant Providence.'

' Don't you mind *her,* my love,' said Lady Madeleine, advancing laughing, and kissing Mrs. Lionel. ' She only means what I do, " welcome." And when she says that you are grown stout, she says the truth ; but if ever she says she is not a Catholic, tell her that she prays for the holy Catholic Church every Sunday.'

With their perfect instinct, so far higher than that wretched humbug called ' tact,'

they had done what they wished to do—
they had put her entirely at her ease.

She took the glass of wine and the biscuit,
and said, with a very pleasant laugh,

'I have been so terribly afraid of coming
near you, but, do you know, I am not in
the least degree afraid of you now.'

'Nobody ever is,' said Lady Madeleine.
'We want to make you really and truly
happy, you know, and we shall easily manage
that.'

Indeed, it was not difficult to be happy
at the Grange, as Mrs. Lionel soon found
out. In a fortnight she was completely one
of the family. No allusions were ever made
as to why she came there, nor were any
allusions made as to how long she was going
to stop there ; save that now and then Lady
Alice or Lady Madeleine would say something of this kind before her,—

'Alice, we will plant this border here by this seat with single daffodils. Mrs. Lionel reads that poem of Wordsworth's very well, and she will like to see some of them next spring. She thought that he meant double-daffodils, foolish thing; we will show her Wordsworth's own.'

'Do you like wallflowers, my love?' Lady Alice would say.

'I like them very greatly,' replied Mrs. Lionel. 'They were a great convent flower.'

'Madeleine,' was the prompt answer, 'we will put those Carter's doubles by her seat. They won't be out till May, Mrs. Lionel, but you will say that there is none like them when they do flower.'

She rested there, in short, and asked no questions,—not even why they, with all their kindness, would call her nothing but Mrs. Lionel, and not by her Christian name.

This place was as sacred, as far as she was concerned, as the convent had been : no one could come near her; and yet there was this difference—she could go anywhere.

Not into the world of crowded streets, not into that miserable, noisy, cruel world which had beat the unfortunate young Irishwoman back to die shipwrecked in the snow at the gates of her own kind convent; but into another one,—the peaceful world of nature, when in her half-subdued or pastoral mood. The two old ladies gave her the key of the postern, and soon found that she had used it, for they watched her like lynxes, with a great unexpressed hope irradiating their two faces when they looked at one another.

Her first expedition was a very short one. She went out at the postern; *they* saw her; but came back in a hurried manner in about twenty minutes, and, locking the door, looked round her as if in relief.

'It is that abominable old noodle Joyce loitering in our back-lane,' said Lady Alice. The fact being that the lane belonged to Joyce, not to them; and so far from loitering, he always went through it with extreme rapidity, lest the devil, which he had once seen in broad sunlight, should step out of the postern, put itself in the pathway between him and his wife, who would face ten devils, and say, 'Joyce, I desire to have a few words with you on the subject of Hephsibah Burton's son. If you refuse me, I shall lay the matter before Mrs. Joyce.' Joyce had a devil in his garden, as well as the old ladies, and *he* never loitered there.

She told Lady Madeleine in confidence that she had gone out, but had been frightened back by something terrible, she knew

not what. It was a thing with great arms
and legs, which roared at her, and which
tossed things wildly about in the air; and
there were wild people about it who seemed
to jeer, and try to murder one another with
weapons; she said that she could not bear
it.

Lady Madeleine told this to Lady Alice;
the latter lady replied—

'You see as well as I do that what has
frightened her is Norris' thrashing machine.
It is very sad that she should be so timid,
but you see, dear, that she has not been out
of a convent for seven years, and she is afraid
of her own shadow when she is alone. It's
that Joyce, of course; it always is: he got
Norris' machine to thrash out his wheat for
his rent. Explain to her what the thing
was, and tell her that it shall never be there
again. Then she will get out on to the

commons and into the lonely lanes, and
begin to talk to the cottagers, and see human
life from the healthy side.   Wotherston,
you and I, and Wilson have agreed to this,
and we are here to see it carried out to its
blessed end.   We shall undo this monstrous
evil in spite of such petty rebuffs as this.'

She went out again after her silly fears
had been explained to her, and every absence
was longer than the last.   She began to ask
simple questions about the peasantry in
the further parts of the parish, towards
the mountain, to which questions she received
voluminous replies; our two ladies knew
these people, and knew uncommonly little
good of some of them, but the evil they kept
to themselves.   They made no enquiries, they
were too shrewd for that, but they noticed
that she almost always brought home flowers
—pinks, sweet Williams, roses, and such

things as grow in cottagers' gardens—they
saw that she was among the poor, and they
desired it.

There was constraint on one point between her and them, for she never spoke of
her husband to them, neither did they just
now desire that she should. Otherwise, with
the exception of the subject of her walks, they
were free. Garden, farm, bees, fruit, flowers,
were quite enough subjects for conversation
in a microcosm like theirs. One morning
at breakfast she asked if Lady Alice could
lend her a Bible. Lady Alice did so with
the most Protestant promptitude, and she
went away down the garden.

'This looks well, Alice,' said Lady Madeleine. 'She is going to read to some sick
person.'

'We shall do it!' said Lady Alice
triumphantly. 'She wanted the world again,

and she is getting the world of God. Now
the fiend take anyone who stops us. May
he be rammed into the great gun of Athlone.'

' I hope she won't turn Protestant,' said
Lady Madeleine dolefully.

' I hope not, I am sure,' said Lady Alice.
'I had as lief you did. I can manage you
now, but I'd never be able to do it then.'

A very little time afterwards Mrs. Lionel
had a consultation on business with the two
ladies. She had a large sum of money in
hand in her desk, but it was all in foreign
notes. Could they oblige her with ten
pounds in English money for some of her
foreign notes?

' Alice is cashier, my love; I am book-
keeper,' said Lady Madeleine.

Lady Alice departed with more alacrity
than she usually did when cash was in
question. The tax collector had very hard

times of it in that house; Lady Alice, though
as loyal a soul as ever stepped, objected to
taxes, and with Irish logic confounded cause
with effect, scolding the agent when she
should have argued with his principal, quar-
relling with the collector when she ought to
have been abusing the Chancellor of the
Exchequer: she never paid her taxes until
threatened with distraint, and appealed as a
matter of course, though she never faced the
Bench. On this occasion, however, she took
the dirty Popish notes without any sign of
disgust, and brought down good English
money for them, nine sovereigns, seventeen
and sixpence in silver, a two-shilling piece,
four pennies, two halfpennies, and four far-
things. Having thus paid off the Pope
without deducting discount, as she expressed
it, and hoping that he would benefit by her
Peter's penny, and think better of his ways,

she left the two other ladies laughing, and
went away.

The next day Mrs. Lionel was a long
time gone, but when she came back she
looked tired, pleased, and happy. She had
in her hand five or six flowers of wild gentianella, of which she took peculiar care, putting them in a glass and carrying them with
her when she went early to bed.

'She has been to the mountain,' said
Lady Madeleine. 'What can she have
wanted there?'

They found out through the footman
they had hired when she was expected, a
younger brother of Gabriel's at Pollington,
and as nimble a spy. They got at it second-
hand of course, but this was the truth.

Up under the mountain lived an out-
rageously disreputable family, who did everything in their small way possible; but none

of whom, the head of the house included, did anything which could be sent for trial : they were a ' six weeks' gang,' the plague of the great unpaid. The head of the house had kicked three policemen, and broken the window of a public-house. The Bench, knowing that he cared nothing for his person, determined to try his pocket, and fined him seven pounds ten, he to be imprisoned until the money was paid. This upset the family calculation altogether; they had the *money*— such people always have ; but, on the one hand, they did not want to pay it, and in winter would have let 'Father' warm his toes in gaol with his full consent. Harvest was coming on, however, and the poaching season to follow. So they were in full committee of ways and means, when Mrs. Lionel passing as far as their cottage under the mountain, heard them squabbling and swearing in the distance, and following that sound of woe to its source, found them all in desolation and tears. To a woman who had been seven years in a convent, their tale of oppression sounded true enough. She paid the money, and 'Father' was let loose on society. The family presented her with the bouquet of gentianella.

'Of course she will make blunders,' said Lady Alice, rubbing her chin. 'But she is going the right way. She is getting used to the world. It will take a long while to undo the work of that scoundrel Cross.'

CHAPTER IV.

SOME ACCOUNT OF DR. CROSS.

WE hope by this time that our readers have become sufficiently interested in Dr. Cross to wish to know something more about him than they have hitherto heard. We knew him very well indeed at one time, before he arrived at the zenith of his fame, which was some time after the period of which we are writing. He is a perfectly real person. We, at one time, in our society, were devoted to him.

The Crosses were not such noodles as to come in with William the Conqueror; they came in with St. Augustine. From the family traditions and from history they proved that St. Augustine never had a sister; a thing never asserted, and therefore one on which they strenuously insisted; but that he had a married aunt with one son. St. Augustine, it appeared from the Cross documents, some as early as the fifteenth century, descended on the barbarian world of Britain, backed by this aunt (and her son). She assisted greatly in the spreading of Christianity by settling in Kent, and buying up every acre of land which she could lay her hands on. She abandoned her Latin name, and took the name of Cross, after the holy symbol, which in her position as aunt to a saint was only natural. The Crosses then became Kings of Kent for many centuries, until deposed by King John. Then their castle at Penshurst was destroyed by Ralf

d'Isle, and all their papers burnt, to the
salvation of the brains of all heralds. They
picked themselves up again at different periods
of history; if ever the name Cross appeared,
he was one of their Crosses; and at last old
Dr. Cross of Brompton paid forty pounds for
his pedigree, and whether from suggestion
or accident found St. Augustine's aunt at the
top of it. This was proof positive. A man
with a clear pedigree for eight hundred
years may make fun of such nonsense, but
there was the fact. Old Dr. Cross thought
himself a greater man than any Howard in
the land.

He kept a little shop in Brompton, a
mean little 'doctor's' shop, having a good
practice, however. On the verge of Chelsea
he had a considerable part of 'Cadogan's
Wilderness,' as it was once called, and not
only made money, but put it by. He was

thought to be a prosperous old fellow, as proud as Lucifer.

His son, John Cross, proved to him, if nothing else could, that there was high blood in the family. We have described him before; we may only add that he was from the first very handsome, and that his manners were perfect, to those who had never seen a gentleman.

I want to see what some have called a 'perfect gentleman.' A man whose cheek never reddens with the eagerness of combat, when another man *rudely* expresses a political opinion contrary to his; a man to whom all religious phases of thought are alike, and who smiles them down, all one after another, in succession; a man who looks upon 'the sex' as being all alike, with no individuality of opinion, or character; a man who says glibly, ' We men

of the world know all about women, and I
assure you that women under no circumstances will ever do '—fifty things which are
done every day by the best of women ; a
man who dashes to open the door with a leer
on his face which he thinks is a smile ; a
man who knows a horse and can ride one,
and will cheat everyone except his friend,
and even him, if there is no chance of being
found out. I will not go on describing the
perfect gentleman, as believed in by some
who know no better : I never met one,
except Dr. Cross.

He was a perfect gentleman in *his*
way,—so perfect, that he was actually believed in by some gentlemen, and a vast
number of middle-class women, whose
brothers and husbands were a million times
better gentlemen than he ever was in
reality.

He went in due season to St. Swithin's
Hospital, a medical school which has always
been supposed to demand the most gentlemanly behaviour on the part of its students ;
but even here he was called ' Gentleman
Cross.' In the way of prizes he carried everything before him, and his conduct was perfectly irreproachable. Genial and kindly, even
to merriment, with his fellow-students, respect-
ful and diligent with superiors, intensely attentive to the patients, he was *at first* one of
the greatest successes ever known. Everybody
was bound to love him. He gained a
scholarship for anatomy, but he refused to
take it, pointing out in the noblest manner
that he was comparatively rich, whereas
Dolly Percy, who had run him so close, was
poor, and needed the money. The Board
had Dolly Percy before them, and dwelling
on the magnanimous conduct of John Cross,

told him that the exhibition was his. To their astonishment and indignation, the offer was refused in the most emphatic manner, and the students gave Dolly Percy a dinner, to which Cross was not invited.

The fact is that although everyone was bound to like Gentleman Cross, no one did after a little; the reason alleged by most of them being that he was *not* a gentleman. He was better looking, better mannered, better dressed, and cleverer than the rest of them; but the young men who afterwards made a mark in the world voted him a 'barber's clerk,' and such was the opinion of their seniors: of this feeling of course the Board knew nothing,

There was something wrong about him, besides the alleged want of human sympathy, though no man liked to give it a name. Theoretically, his knowledge of medicine was sublime for his age, but in practice his

luck seemed to desert him. The students
said that he had no feeling for any individual
patient, and treated them all as an old-
fashioned vet. would treat a horse; the
professors said (after he was safe off the
premises) that he was a trifle rash and
Frenchy in the exhibition of certain drugs.
One physician said that it would be lucky if
Cross was never indicted for manslaughter ;
a savage and untameable old surgeon, who
never gave a civil word to any human being
except his poorest patients, and who was
adored by everyone about the place, from
the necessary savage who in those days
provided for science in the dissecting room
up to the most cantankerous member of
the Board, said that the puppy would be
hanged, and the sooner the better : the hemp,
however, was not sown which would hang
John Cross.

His father died, and left him all his money: we do not know how much that was. John, now Dr. Cross, knew the value of money pretty well, and he considered it to be enough to furnish a house in Bolton Row, and put up a new brass plate: his father's shop, fixtures, and goodwill he sold to a young man for six hundred pounds. One of his enemies said that this was the only money he ever had, but we are very strongly inclined to doubt that. John Cross was a man whose more intimate acquaintances (such as he had) used always to get at the truth by believing exactly the contrary of everything he said: had he said he was rich, they would have believed him poor, and *rice rersâ*. On this subject, however, he never said anything at all. The reader may make him rich or poor, as his fancy dictates.

He had not calculated his resources badly

by any means. Immediately after his appearance in Bolton Row there occurred a
peculiarly acrimonious squabble between
the Board and the staff of the old hospital,
which ultimately led to the secession of the
chairman on the one side, and the untameable surgeon on the other, after high and
unforgivable words. The Duke was in the
right; he had discovered that there was
waste in a particular manner, which his
eagle eye alone had discovered. The old
surgeon allowed the fact, after examination,
but said that the Duke had got his information from a charlatan. The affair heated
itself, and the quarrel, so cleverly originated
(though no one dreamt of it) by Cross, took
a party phase. The Duke shook the dust
off his feet after resigning, without giving
the name of his informant; and the surgeon,
after telling such of the Board as had sup-

ported the Duke that they might all go to the devil, departed also to the intense grief of the whole establishment—including the body-snatcher, who wept like a child.

However, Cross had got what he wanted ; he always got everything he wished for : only one thing was beyond his reach, the love of his fellow-men, and that he did not care for. Popularity he wanted, and got ; but the only being who ever loved him heartily was that poor dumb dog Arthur Branscombe. Cross, I say, had got what he wanted now : the Duke took him up, and gave him introductions.

He had been looking his chances in the face, and if he had not secured the Duke his intention had been to start as an homœopathist, but he knew that to step between the Duke and his blue pills would be ruin in a social point of view ; and besides, he argued

scientifically, 'That man has assimilated such
a quantity of calomel now that he would die
without it; and I want him to live until I
have done with him.'   He therefore took all
the homœopathist books, which he had very
carefully read up with a view to starting in
that line himself, and made a ferocious attack
on them in an able pamphlet.   Pamphlets
as a rule do not sell, but this one did, for
there were deliciously cutting personal on-
slaughts on the leading homœopathists by
name which made the thing go off like wild-
fire.   There are charlatans everywhere, and
one of the homœopathists of those times
happened not to have 'a clean bill of health;'
this Cross knew, and by the expenditure of
a few pounds hunted up the man's antece-
dents, and used the shortcomings of the
individual for the purpose of holding the
whole system up to scorn.   What connec-

tion there was between infinitesimal doses
and the fact of a man's having been imprisoned abroad for using *juniperus sabiensis*
unsuccessfully the illogical public did not
seek to enquire : the pamphlet was spicy and
personal, and it put that guardian of the
people, Dr. Cross, before the public. Burstenberg, the only queer man among the
homœopathists, was the most tender about
his character : in the case of ' Burstenberg
versus Cross,' a British jury valued his
character at one farthing. He went into
business in the city (with the farthing we
suppose), did well, and built a church.

Cross and he were afterwards very great
friends, for Burstenberg had more experience
in irregular practice than Cross, and was a
thorough-going scoundrel, necessary therefore
to Cross, who was always eminently respectable.
' I would give you a hundred pounds,' said

Cross once to Burstenberg, 'if you would give me your trick of lying, and looking honest at the same time.' But this was beyond the art of Burstenberg. He said that it was an affair of national genius, and that the English were fools.

Cross naturally agreed with Burstenberg that the English were fools; but at the same time he saw that the German folly would no more last than the Scotch folly, or the French folly. He wanted to see a sound system of English medicine, with Dr. Cross at the head of it.

We can say nothing except that he partially succeeded. He had a start such as few men get, and he made the best of it. The older hands said among themselves that he was a charlatan: but who would bell the cat? Not one. The men who would call him a charlatan behind his back, were forced to confess him one of the ablest living physicians before his face. He was a man very much sought after also. Some coroners did not find themselves safe without him. On one occasion a coroner quoted Dr. Taylor. 'He is obsolete,' said Dr. Cross; and the coroner was satisfied.

He had, in not very many years, dropped into a considerable practice. I wish to say as little as possible about the man's ways and means. But his bankers were rather astonished at the amount of some of his fees: they were larger than Sir James Simpson's. That, of course, was no business of the bankers, for he always kept a large balance. Bankers, however, have their ideas; and if John Cross had wished to overdraw, in all probability he would not have been allowed to do so.

We hope that we have now given a

sufficient account of Dr. Cross, and his relations with that part of the world in which I
hope we all live—the respectable. Dr.
Cross was pre-eminently respectable, but the
respectable world, proverbially stupid, did
not see their way to the fact. The women
had nothing to say against him, but the
idiotic men were as usual in the way—they
did not like Dr. Cross. One or two of them
went so far as to propose to throw Dr. Cross
out of the window—had they done so, the
laws of their country would have hanged
them. We live among formulas, and by
formulas: one of them is that you should
not throw a man to whom you object out of
window. You could not do it, in the first
place; and in the second place, if you did
throw him out of window, or downstairs,
you might be tried for your life, and it
would go hard with you. Some people

threatened to horsewhip Cross—no one ever did so effectually. A young man certainly once hit Cross over the shoulder with a whip, and told him to consider himself horsewhipped; but Cross answered by two terrible blows on the young man's eyes, and had him up at Marlborough Street before he was presentable. He was asked about the cause of the quarrel, but he would say nothing. Cross had calculated on that among other things.

We cannot follow him in his career with any amount of detail: the man had a splendidly solid foundation of science, and he used it until he gained technical knowledge of a certain nature, such as was possessed by no man out of France. In certain cases the untameable old surgeon, whilome of St. Swithin's, would call him in, and he would not always come.

He was not so prosperous that he was
beyond the *idea* of marrying a woman with
a handsome fortune.   He hated and despised
women, certainly; they were to him an
inferior animal; by some ridiculous tradition,
probably Biblical, allowed to possess property.   If he could get hold of a woman
with property, he would have no funda-
mental objection to marrying her, and determined not to ill-use her.   Still he was on
the whole averse to marriage.   He had seen,
in his opinion, too much of it among other
people; he had seen various relations between married people, and none of them
appeared satisfactory; he went through the
old Pantagruel and Panurge Matrimonial
Catechism with himself, and his answer was
a decided negative to matrimony, unless he
could get all he wanted, and he hardly knew
what that was.

A poor woman, however pretty, was out of the question : he, although prosperous, could not afford that : a pretty and rich woman might be tolerable, yet even there were difficulties : she might be clever and determined, which would not do, for he was determined to be master ; she might be an obedient fool, in which case she would not be of any great use to him : his wife must be clever and obedient at the same time. She must have perfect temper too, for he had a temper himself which sometimes made him angry with the person he loved best in the world (that is to say John Cross), and how were you to know what a woman's temper was until you were shut up with her without hope of release? And there might be children, again ; and if there was one set of people in the world whom Cross hated, it was children, though they with their usual

correctness of instinct adored him, and de-
tested the savage old surgeon whom all
grown-up people reverenced. Cross sometimes, in his day-dreams, would fancy that
he was married to a woman old enough to
be his mother, with forty thousand pounds
settled on him, who doted on him: but then,
suppose that she was religious? Good
heavens! No, Cross was fairly on his way
to being a confirmed bachelor, when Lord St.
Augustine died, leaving no known heirs.

Such a chance for an advertisement was
not to be lost. Cross instantly claimed and
assumed the title, sent orders to the tenants
on the entailed estates to pay their rents to
his solicitors, and, had there been much
available property, might have got into
serious financial trouble. Whether he ever
believed himself to be the real man or not,
he was not likely to tell anybody; whether

it was merely an advertising scheme, we cannot say. He was cautious enough never to take any of the rents from the strictly entailed property, but Lord St. Augustine he was for above six weeks. Unfortunately for him, the estates, though small, were worth contesting. Messrs. Decker and Herne, a very old firm of solicitors, after due incubation, produced a man—their own out-door young man—and fought Cross with him. Had it not been for the fact that this young man had drifted into an attorney's office, Cross might have been Lord St. Augustine. But this young man had spoken of his parentage more than once, and his employers thought Cross's claim so exceedingly impudent, that they had examined into that of their out-door clerk: the result was that they started their man at once. Cross, taken by surprise, lost his head, and con-

tested as long as his money lasted: when he
was left without a stiver, he gracefully gave
in.   Whether the present Lord has any real
title to the estates we know not—the
House of Lords decided he had more than
Cross which was sufficient.   The Peerage
has, to its great surprise, gained a most
admirable recruit in the person of the penni-
less clerk, who has won golden opinions;
and it has been saved from Cross.

He had to look about him now to recruit;
his practice had gained, but his fortune,
whatever it may have been, was gone.   He
determined to marry, and he looked about
for a rich wife: he was by no means so
particular as he had once been.   Edith
Seton, though poor, had very large prospects
of succession.   They might come sooner or
later, but they were certain, and money could
be raised upon them.   Edith Seton then

must marry John Cross, *faute de mieux*, and if he wanted money he must raise it on her estate. No human being could keep her out of 16,000*l.*, and she would probably have far more if a certain uncle did not alter his will. She would *do*. She must be Mrs. Cross, poor as she was at present.

CHAPTER V.

A FEW WORDS MORE ABOUT CROSS.

EDITH SETON was convent-bred, in the
strictest sense, and was a patient of Dr.
Cross, as was also her aunt and natural
guardian, Lady Longmynd, Lady Madeleine
Howard's sister : the girl was an orphan,
rather dazed with the world, and it was not
very difficult for Cross to gain an over-
whelming influence over her. Her health
was weak at the time, and Cross carefully
terrified her and Lady Longmynd on the
subject. No look or gesture of his ever
showed that he was anything more than

scientifically interested in his patients, but his assiduity was so great that it gave rise to alarm, and indeed Edith did not seem to improve at all, but grew very low and hysterical. A feeble girl out of a convent, frightened with the world, was not difficult to manage by Cross, and he felt pretty sure of his game. His expectations, however, were all dashed to the ground.

If he had been anyone else, he would have blown his brains out for his insensate folly. Had his brains been anyone else's, they would certainly have been in jeopardy; but being John Cross's brains, and serviceable to John Cross, they were allowed to remain where they were. He would have cursed himself, but being an atheist he had nothing to curse by, and so was denied even that relief to his feelings. He could feel astonished contempt for himself, but that was not consoling.

He fell in love with the girl. We blush as we write down this weakness on the part of our friend Dr. Cross, but such was undoubtedly the case. He told the fact to Arthur Branscombe—or rather to the furniture, of which Arthur Branscombe formed the most insignificant item—one night at Pollington. And poor Arthur, who never forgot anything in the long run, told the whole of this conversation, and many other things also, some time afterwards, and was about three weeks in doing it.

Lord Longmynd was a singularly shrewd person, who agreed with every proposition made to him in his household, but who seldom opened his mouth except to give an order, frequently in direct contradiction of what the female part of his house considered to be his intentions. When he announced one morning, therefore, that he was going to Italy, everybody knew that to Italy they were going, and made the best of it, which was not very bad after all.

He was greatly devoted to Edith, and was getting alarmed about her health. He did not understand Cross, and seldom having had need of a doctor himself, had little idea of his abilities. But the untameable surgeon happened to be a friend of his, and he went to him at one o'clock one day, when his patients had departed, and consulted him about Edith.

The great surgeon heard everything, and was prepared with the immediate and, in his opinion, certain remedy of kicking Cross out of the house, or getting the grooms to do it : he remarked that it would take more than one. This, however, was obviously impossible; and after much bad language he gave it as his opinion that the best thing would be to take the girl to Italy.

'The scoundrel can't follow her there, you know, Longmynd,' he said; 'and if he does, you could have him poisoned for four hundred scudi. I would gladly give double the money if——.'

'If what?' said Lord Longmynd.

'If I knew as much as he does,' said the surgeon, looking at him steadily.

Cross's prey was snatched from his grasp. There were plenty of other women with whom he might have had a chance: alas for him, he loved only this one. The arrow of that wretched, naked, blind imp had hit him between the joints of the harness, and he was left as love-sick (that we should say so!) as the greatest noodle of a boy who had consulted him when he considered himself dying of that complaint, and to whom Cross had prescribed his usual *remedium amoris*, seeing the world,—in other words, dissipation.

Worse befell him, however. Edith Seton had always been told, even before she left the convent, that she would some day have to marry some man or another. She had accepted this as her fate, and had been gravely rebuked for remarking, in recreation, what a delightful arrangement it would be if the Archbishop would marry them all (by ' all ' she meant the Lady Superior, nine nuns, and twenty-five *élèves*) and save further trouble. The good old man laughed till the tears ran down his cheeks when the scandalized Lady Superior told him this, and said that he was fifty years too old to think of such a thing. In fact, Edith had not the remotest notion about marrying or falling in love. She liked the Archbishop best, then

Dr. Cross, and she probably would have accepted Lord Longmynd, in gratitude for his
protection, only there was Lady Longmynd.

At Florence she met some one who, after
the very first interview, seemed to her in
some way different to the Archbishop, to
Cross, or to Lord Longmynd. 'You turn
out nature by every means, but she always
comes back.'

To Edith at Naples appeared a young
man. She did not feel inclined to go down
on her knees to him, as she did to the
Archbishop; she was not afraid of him, as
she was of Dr. Cross; and she did not think
him to be the most estimable of men, as she
did Lord Longmynd. There was a *specialité*
about this young man which she had never
seen in any other.

She wondered when he was coming, and
she wondered why he went away. They

did not speak much to one another, and
when they did his French was not good,
and her English not perfect. But there is
a peculiar language which must have been
spoken in Eden (for which idea I am indebted
to the author of 'Elsie Venner'); and the
convent-bred Edith and the public school-
bred Lionel both knew it, though neither of
them had ever talked it before. It was the
curious language of love.

No difficulty was thrown in their way.
Lionel Branscombe was a very eligible match
in every way: he was young, handsome,
tolerably rich. He was so well thought of
by the powers that be, that he had been
requested to assist in a somewhat delicate
affair, though he did not regularly belong
to the diplomatic service. He held much
such a position as the late Lord Zouch did at
one time, and people said that he was cut

out for a colonial governor at the very least; but it was thought that he flew at higher game than that, and that he aimed at a high place in the imperial councils, some said the highest.

Edith Seton was his second cousin, and no actual blood-relation to him. She had, as we have previously mentioned, no immediate dowry, and Lionel knew less about her expectations than Cross. They were married, everything having been settled on her, and for some time nothing occurred to mar the harmony of their lives.

But if Lionel thought that he could thwart Cross in the dearest wish of his heart, without being made to feel it, he was utterly mistaken.

Lionel was the most devoted of husbands, and she the most loving of wives. His friends said among one another that

she was a fool, but this was not entirely true;
everybody except Lionel saw that she was
hopelessly ignorant in the ways of the world,
and that she was by no means the sort of
wife for a rising young politician. She made
blunders about people in the world, and was,
politically speaking, hopelessly indiscreet.
Romanism was not then fashionable, in fact
was pre-eminently unfashionable, and so her
creed did her husband very little good.
What Lionel's creed was he would have been
somewhat puzzled to tell you. Not very
strong on any point; so liberal that he would
have laughed even at Wotherston had he
warned him against marrying a Roman
Catholic. This, Wotherston did not do, as
he was perfectly aware that it would have
been useless; and, besides, Wotherston had
seen Clara before her entry into the world,
and had given his heart to her.

Lionel had, in his first dream of love, looked for a return of that unbounded confidence which he gave his wife : he found that there was a third person in the house who came between them, and was more important than he was—the priest. This was a great jar to him ; but he pretended that he did not care for it ; and speaking to Wotherston once about the matter, Wotherston told him he had no power of complaint, for that he had married with his eyes open. He knew everything about the use of confession in the Romish Church ; he had married a Roman Catholic, and now had no right to say a word against his wife's religion.

This was undoubtedly true ; but it did not prevent furious jealousy on his part against the priest. A wise priest of a certain type would in all probability have directed, recommended, or whatever it is

called, Edith Branscombe to tell the whole
truth to her husband at once. I fancy that
even that peculiarly unscrupulous little fellow,
Father Wilson, would certainly have done
so, and gained Lionel's confidence, gratitude,
and vote in the House of Commons for ever.
But Edith Branscombe's director, in spite of
his agreeable manners, was a low, blundering
hound, without the wits of a second-class
lawyer's clerk. He had some muddy idea
that it would be well to stand between Edith
and her heretic husband, whom he described
as being doomed to perdition; and some
letters which were addressed to her were
carefully concealed from Lionel. This man
was like wax in the hands of Cross, who
very quickly made *his* acquaintance; and
anyone who knew Cross might be sure,
that to the question 'Quis dirigit ipsos
directores?' the answer would be Cross

and his dear friend Burstenberg, the latter
of whom was not as yet above dirty work.
Most gradually, most carefully, and most
slowly was the mine laid under Lionel's
feet. The soul which directed the plot or
mine was that of Cross; the brain which
elaborated the details was that of Burstenberg; and the hand which executed it was
that of Edith Branscombe's director.

One would fancy that a plot with three
people in it would be pretty certain to fail;
generally that is the case, but not always.
The present writer found himself once in the
middle of one of the most insane political
plots which ever troubled Europe, as *he*
thought. The most ridiculous thing was
that the plotters thought him, the present
writer, a man to be of some importance.
The present writer protested that he did
not know, or wish to know, anything about

the plot; but they insisted on taking him into their counsels. He never did anything towards the matter; and yet a certain king is on the throne now. The plot succeeded to the unutterable surprise of your humble servant, who afterwards discovered that more people knew of it than he did. This, however, is beyond the mark—is only an exception to prove the rule. All the writer intends is this, that a good plot should have only two people in it, not three. The Fenians, for example, might have made the most infernal mischief if they had not had a public organ : Cross, in his plot against Lionel Branscombe, never showed his hand, but possessed his soul in peace.

Little by little Lionel Branscombe saw that the gentle winning love which he had first had from his wife was being replaced by an odd nervous terror. He spoke to her

about it, but she never really answered him.
She denied the fact; and then what could
he possibly do? He redoubled his attentions, and she seemed to reciprocate them.
Yet he saw that there was something beyond
his power of removal. He was never rude
or harsh with her, but she was evidently
terrified by his presence. Confidence between them he now knew was impossible,
—the priest had proved that to him; but he
would have laid himself at her feet, with the
priest between them, if he could have got
back the old girl love and confidence.

It was not to be. The conspirators
played their game too well. Lionel was
fond of physical science,—that was found
out; and the most plausible Burstenberg
made his acquaintance. Edith was very
much attached to a Polish cousin of hers,
and he was utilised to provoke Lionel's

jealousy. She was with him very often—
more often than Lionel cared for. But this
matter of jealousy was by no means Cross's
trump card.

She was steadily brought to believe—a
thing not very difficult—that Lionel thought
her to be *légère*. At the same time Burstenberg was doing his share; he had cast
homœopathy to the winds as far as infinitesimal doses went, but he stuck to it in
principle. 'Similia similibus curantur' was
always in his mouth. A very little Latin
may do a vast deal of mischief. The simple
word 'Filioque' has set Christendom by the
ears, to the great wonder of the Turks; and
when ordinary English people asked Burstenberg for a proof of his theory about the
hair of the dog which bit you, he was ready
with his Latin, and shut them up.

This very clever scoundrel got hold of

Lionel by Cross's directions. Burstenberg
at that time had not got any money; Cross
had; he had always money coming in, in
rather large fees. The end of the whole
business was that Cross was entirely successful. A child was born to Lionel and
Edith. It was a year old when Edith, we
will not say was ordered to go, but at all
events *went* into *retraite* at her old convent,
without speaking to her husband about the
matter, and was accompanied by her young
cousin the Pole. The child was left at
Highgate, and sickened by some trifling
disease. Lionel was detained in London on
parliamentary business, when the news of
the child's illness was brought to him by
Burstenberg, whom he himself had asked to
go to Highgate. Burstenberg and he consulted together, and thought that from the
symptoms the child should have calomel.

The friendly Burstenberg went up to Highgate with the calomel, and Lionel rode up
to see his child early the next morning.

The child was dead!

Nothing could possibly be more simple
than the whole affair; nothing more natural.
Edith had possibly gone *en retraite* without
consulting Lionel, and had accepted the
escort of her cousin, for whose attentions she
did not particularly care. Lionel had bought
a small dose of calomel at a shop, and sent
it up by the friendly Burstenberg to Highgate. The poor child died, as children will,
whether well or ill treated. Is there anything improbable in that?

What did Cross and his emissaries make
of it? It is astonishing what a congeries of
scoundrels can make out of nothing. Lionel
was first maddened by being made to believe
that Edith had left him, and secondly that

he had killed his own child. Edith was made to think that Lionel believed in her guilt, and had poisoned the child in revenge. With a master-mind such as that of Cross, such things are not difficult. All which such men require to work upon are honest people who will believe every word they say : having known Cross, we know that we are writing very much within the truth.

The infinity of mischief which may be made by an unscrupulously respectable man is hardly calculable. We do not believe that Cross ever intended that Lionel should have fought the lamentable duel which ruined him for a time. It is enough that he did so. That every explosive force was exercised against him; that he and Edith were made to believe lies, by people better in possession of facts than they were themselves; that the suspicion engendered by a foolish priest

had its fruit; that Lionel suspected Edith,
and Edith Lionel—why go on—unless one
would refuse the reader all powers of imagi-
nation? A hopeless scoundrel like Cross, a
charlatan like Burstenberg, and a Roman
priest like Edith's director were agreed, and
Lionel and Edith retired from the world.
Enough has been said about their way of
doing so.

Lionel Branscombe had come in Cross's
way, and he was very soon made to know
the fact.

Years went on, and Cross never very
much troubled himself about Lionel. He
considered that he had inflicted sufficient
injury on him. By degrees, too, the love he
had conceived for Edith died out, and he
wondered that he had ever been such a
fool.

Accident had cast him in the way of

Arthur Branscombe, and possibly some
reminiscence of Edith made him less reck-
less to him than he was to others. I say
possibly, because Cross was a man who
spared no one. To Arthur Branscombe he
behaved as though he contemptuously liked
him : Arthur soon began to revere him as
a kind of divine scoundrel—the sort of man
he would like to be himself, if he had the
brains.

CHAPTER VI.

STRUAN TAKES THE SHOOTING AT POLLINGTON.

'MR. STRUAN,' said Arthur at breakfast, the morning after his arrival, 'I have had a letter from my brother, which I should like to read to you.'

'Would it not be better to read it to Dr. Cross?' said Mr. Struan. 'I really do not wish to meddle with your affairs : I have nothing to do with the relations between yourself and your brother Lionel, for I suppose that it is he to whom you allude.'

Arthur remained silent for some time, and then he said,

'There were many fellows worse than my governor.'

As this was in all probability true, Struan did not contradict Arthur: the remark had nothing to do with the matter; but Struan knew perfectly well that Arthur would speak to the purpose sooner or later; and so he let him be, and took another cup of coffee.

Arthur took up the subject, whatever it was, at an entirely new place. He was always under the impression that his listener was following him through his involved reasonings. Struan knew this, and was not in the least degree surprised when Arthur said,

'It appears that it is all lies to say that Charlemagne was a Frenchman; he was a German, like that man Burstenberg.'

Had he not been so attentive to his egg,

he would have seen a sharp look in Struan's
eyes. But he saw nothing.

'The letter I got from my brother Lionel
this morning,' said Arthur, after some time,
'is dated from Brussels—where he seems to
be at large. My brother, as I have previously explained to you, is a lunatic, and I
want to shut him up: partly because I dis-
like his drawing any more money, and partly
that there are very heavy charges hanging
over his head. But the odd thing is that he
does not write like a lunatic at all. I *wish*
you would read the letter.'

'Hand it to me, then,' said Struan.

He ran his eye over it for a decent time,
and returned it ; we may be more polite to
it than he was, and give it *in extenso.*

'My dear Arthur,—You would not know
me if you saw me, I dare say ; but we were

never enemies. I am now told by those who never deceive me, that after having left me alone for some years, you are taking a course violently antagonistic to me. I would ask you why you should do so? I never offended you: I never had the chance of doing so.

'You propose to prove me a lunatic; you might as well try to prove the Prime Minister to be one. You have no hope there. If I were to come forward to-morrow before the Lord Chancellor, you would be utterly beaten. I have more brains than you have, my poor Arthur, or possibly than any of your advisers.

'Why do I not come forward? you ask. Arthur, things have happened in my life which I cannot contemplate even now with equanimity. I was mad (in one sense) when I killed a perfectly honest and innocent man. I think that I was mad when I believed that

I killed my own child. All this has been, I
begin to believe, a monstrous folly concerted
by scoundrels.

'I pray only one thing of you, to leave
my ruined life where it is, and not to drag it
before the public. Surely, for the sake of
our father, to whose memory you have been
so faithful, you will do that much for me.

'LIONEL BRANSCOMBE.'

'What do you think of that?' said
Arthur.

'It hardly seems the letter of a madman,'
replied Struan. 'I have before told you that
I knew your brother, and am his friend. Do
you not think, in a matter of such delicacy,
that you should consult your brother George?'

This astounding proposition completely
upset Arthur's reason for a long time. His
coffee grew cold while he stared at Struan,

who took not the slightest notice. Struan
was the sharpest fellow that Arthur had ever
met, except Cross, and he had proposed
taking George into their counsels on a very
delicate matter. If Struan had proposed that
George should have gone to Newmarket to
get a safe tip, Arthur would have pointed
out that his brother would be the very
best man for the purpose, but that it would
not be safe to pay him his honorarium
until after the event. But the taking of
George into his counsels had never occurred
to him.

The outcome of his long cogitation was
this :

'But George is such a thundering queer
fellow, and he has not got any money.'

'I grant both positions at once,' said
Struan; 'but your brother has a singularly
keen brain, and I think it might be useful to

you. He is not at breakfast this morning, I notice.'

'No, I sent him away, so that I might talk to you,' said Arthur, telling the truth first, and then trying to lie it down. 'I mean that he is driving one of the horses for me. But do you really think that we ought to consult him?'

'He is your brother and your heir. No one has more right to be consulted.'

'Then,' said Arthur, 'I will send for him;' and in a wonderfully short space of time George appeared.

He had been contending with horses for two or three hours, but his dress was perfect. The beautiful lithe clean-limbed scoundrel stepped up to the breakfast table and stood between Arthur and Struan, putting his hand on the table-cloth, and looking straight at Struan, who steadily returned his gaze.

Had anyone save Arthur been in the
room, they would have noticed that Struan
in an accidental manner laid his hand on
George's, and that George never removed
his.

'You have ordered me in from the stable,'
he said, 'where I am employed in breaking
your horses, and have no authority over your
grooms. What do you want with me?'

This was extremely disconcerting to
Arthur, but he picked up his brains with
remarkable rapidity. He said, 'We wish to
consult you about Lionel.'

'Consult *me*,' said George. 'Rather late
in the day, is it not? Besides, I have given
you my advice before. Lionel ought to be
locked up in Bedlam, and the accumulation
of his income set aside for Cross. I said
that before, under dictation. What am I to
say now? I'll say anything I am paid to

say, but I like the money first. When I
have got the money,' he went on rather
hurriedly, 'I always speak the truth, and I
am going to speak the truth now. I think
that Lionel ought to be left alone. He never
did *us* any harm. This is exactly the contrary to my previous advice, but I speak as
I am paid : I mean, I speak as I think. A
fellow thinks one thing at one time and
another at another. Have I said what you
wished, Mr. Struan ? '

' Quite so,' said Struan.

' Then I will go back to my horses,' said
George. ' If that brother of mine were to
die, I should be master of everything here.
I call you to witness, Mr. Struan, as a man
respected by both of us, that nothing stands
between me and prosperity but that man's
life, who frequently treats me like a dog, and
at this moment is staring at us both like the

moonstruck idiot which he is. I have been
ordered off the Heath, Mr. Struan ; I have
been expelled my clubs ; and I am a lost
man socially ; but I would risk—aye, and do
risk—my life for that man. His mother was
mine, and I would do that much for him.
Look at him, Mr. Struan—look at the be-
sotted noodle. Why, if I were to die for
that fellow to-morrow, he would not smoke
one cigar the less. And he calls himself my
brother. Bah !'

With which brotherly speech George
departed. Arthur gave Struan a cigar, lit
one himself, and after a time said,

'My brother George is given to scolding.
I noticed the same thing in my mother.
George takes after his mother, and scolds ;
now I take after the governor, and don't
mind it. The governor would stand a couple
of hours' scolding so long as he couldn't

catch hold of anything handy to shy at her. And my mother could dodge neater than I have ever seen any woman do. Lord bless you, my mother would see a book coming at the length of the room. As for fireirons, she always took them away before she began. My mother was a very remarkable woman, Mr. Struan.'

Struan saw that Arthur was excited, as far as he could be, by George's ferocity, and was inclined to talk : he therefore smoked and listened. The first part of Arthur's discourse was by no means promising. But Struan had his ends to gain and was patient.

' James Jarvis,' said Arthur, ' caught the lumbago by sitting in the wet breaking stones at fifty shillings the measured yard, in the wettest autumn the governor ever remembered in his lifetime. It is therefore

absolute nonsense to sow your house peas in
November, for do what you will you will
never gather before May 25, even with
Sutton's Early Champion or Sangster's No. 1.
That shows the folly of some people. You
see what I mean, don't you?'

'Yes,' said Struan.

'It is exactly as I told you then. My
governor was not born on Saturday night,
and he told me that Lady Alice Brown was
in love with Lord Algy Howard. Well,
Lady Madeleine — his sister and she you
know—go off and shut themselves up, for
ever so many years.'

'Now,' continued Arthur to Struan,
'Lionel has been a great fool; but it does
not follow that he is to be locked up.
Lionel might have been Prime Minister, but
he threw the whole thing to the winds. He
poisoned his child, and shot Vambersasky,

—devil of a name that,—six foot one; invented the electric telegraph, you know.'

'I thought Cook and Wheatstone had done that,' said Struan.

'No,' said Arthur; 'I knew Coke of Holkam,—they pronounce their name Cook. You are wrong in your man.—Coke's father was not the man who invented the electric telegraph; he invented the Leicester mutton. *Eighty—pound—a—quarter!* and not such a bad staple of wool, I should say. I have had an eight pound fleece from one of them, with a length of seven inches. Well, that leads up to what I was telling you about; that Clara, my sister, got engaged to Wotherston.'

'Exactly,' says Struan, seeing that his only hope was letting Arthur go his own road; for if he had stopped him there would certainly have been a pause of half an hour.

'Now Edith my brother Lionel's wife,
was a very different person to Clara. She
was a Roman Catholic, but she didn't like
me for all that.'

There was such an awful gap between
cause and effect here, that Struan asked
him to repeat what he had just said.
Arthur supplied the hiatus in this very singular way after a long pause.

'She had been engaged to be married to
Cross before she ever saw Lionel, and she
pitched Cross overboard because Lionel's
prospects were better.'

An exclamation which sounded to
Arthur's practised ears singularly like 'dam-
nation,' rang through the room. Struan was
ill again, and deadly pale. Arthur rose to
the situation.

'You had much better let me put the
knife into that sebaceous tumour of yours,

Struan. I would do it for you as neat as ninepence.'

But Struan did not desire this attention. He rose steadily, and leaning his back against the chimney-piece, said,

'My dear Mr. Branscombe, I must take you partially into my confidence: that is only just to you. I am an old, and intimate friend of your brother Lionel's and of Wotherston's. I am here in Lionel's interests. The exclamation which I uttered just now was not caused by pain, but by the extreme surprise which it gave me to hear that any close relation had existed between Mrs. Lionel and Dr. Cross. I humbly apologise for the words I used.'

'There was only one,' said Arthur; 'and as for that, you wouldn't think much of it if you lived in the house with George when he is out of cash. You should hear *him*.'

'But do you conceive that there was ever anything between Mrs. Lionel Branscombe and Dr. Cross?' asked Struan.

'That I can't tell you anything at all about,' said Arthur. 'She was not fond of me, and women are very curious; I only know what Burstenberg told me. Now Burstenberg is as great a blackguard as George, only he is not such a perfect gentleman: that is what I admire in my brother, with all his faults; he is a real gentleman. I never was. No more was the governor.'

'Now to change the subject, my dear Mr. Branscombe,' said Struan. 'Do you care about your shooting?'

'George does the shooting,' said Arthur. 'I don't shoot well. George kills the game, and I give him a quarter of it to sell: it is cheaper than playing cards with him, for you never know where George will have

you. The people about here don't ask me
out shooting much, because they say that I
hit all their birds and miss my own. If you
like to go shooting here you can : George will
swear confoundedly, but he always does that.'

'What I mean is simply this,' said
Struan ; 'will you let your shooting to me
and let me board here ? Such an arrangement is not unusual in a bachelor's establishment like yours. I would give two
hundred a year, paid in advance.'

'I should not mind it at all.' said Arthur.
'I should have the benefit of your society,
and you would not mind George when you
got used to him. I think that I would say
yes.'

Struan left the room and came back
with a cheque for the money : a business-like
promptitude which excited Arthur's admira-
tion.

George came in from the stables not long after, and looked hungrily at the table; but Arthur had for once, at all events, been thoughtful; he rang the bell and ordered Mr. George's breakfast. Gabriel came in with hot coffee, kidneys, and what not, and George sat down. He did not say grace— he never did; but there was a stealthy, not unkindly look at his brother from his fox-like eyes, which pleased Struan better than the most elaborate grace could have done. It caused him to say to himself,

'There is good to be done here, even with these two savages. After all they are brothers. God speed me!'

CHAPTER VII.

GABRIEL DEPARTS.

GEORGE BRANSCOMBE was known among his numerous sporting friends as a ' straight tip when it was worth his while.' This launches us on seas of speculation as to what sort of person an unstraight or crooked tip must be. His tip or prophecy that Cross would turn up on wheels proved to be singularly correct; but then he had no one to bet with on the event except the grooms, and they would not trust him. Otherwise he might have made what he called a nice little thing of it. A fly was seen driving up the avenue the next morning; and George, seeing business slipping away from under his nose, offered desperately to bet Struan six to one that Cross was in it. Struan did not invest his money, and Cross was · safely deposited at the door—more safely possibly than if George had been driving.

'I wish I had the driving of the beggar,' he said to Struan, as they stood in the window looking at the unconscious Cross, paying the young man who had driven him over. 'I'd bump him. I wish I could get him behind Chanticleer: I'd take my chance of a broken collarbone, and a row with Arthur for smashing his best brougham. I know *that.*'

'Yet you put me behind Chanticleer, and let the groom drive,' said Struan.

'But I put myself behind him too, Mr.

Struan,' said George simply. 'Both our eggs were in the same basket.'

'You would have sold me that horse, you know, George Branscombe,' said Struan.

' Well, what is a beggar to do who hasn't got any money? I shouldn't be any worse than anybody else if I could get money without a row. You pay me handsomely, and I do the handsome thing by you; you can't deny that.'

'Why, no,' said Struan, laughing. ' I am satisfied for the present. I wish you would do right for its own sake.'

' I can't afford it,' said George; and Dr. Cross entered the room.

He certainly *was* a splendid-looking man. Struan was obliged to confess that, though he did not like him. His dress, too, was as perfect as Struan's; and there was a frank, honest, genial *bonhomie* about the man

which made Struan admire him, though he
knew his man tolerably, for his friend George
had told him a great deal, and in doing so
had naïvely told Struan that he always could
tell the truth if he was paid, whereas Cross
could not.

'I am delighted to see you here, Mr.
Struan,' said Cross, 'for Pollington is not
lively now. George, my dear fellow, how
are you?'

'*I'm* very well,' said George; 'so is
Arthur. The bay colt has got the colic: I
wish you would see to him.'

George had been requested to be civil to
Cross by head-quarters; this was a speci-
men of his tender mercies in the way of
civility. He got a look from Struan which
he well understood, and before Cross had
time to say anything in reply to the deadly
insult he went on :

'I really wish to heaven you would : you might save Arthur a couple of hundred. Since he has taken to do his own vet. business, I am obliged to ask such friends of the family as are left for assistance. Mr. Struan here has been giving me advice.'

'I'll see the horse,' said Cross with the most perfect apparent good-humour, wishing that George was ill, and that he had the doctoring of him, just as George wished that the Doctor wanted to go from one place to another, and that he had the driving of him.

'I hope you have come for a good long visit, Dr. Cross,' said Struan.

'I don't know exactly how long I shall stay,' said Cross. 'My professional duties may call me away at any time. Do you stay any time in this part of the country ?'

'I shall be at Pollington about three months, I fancy.'

Cross was taken by surprise for once in his life.

'Three months!' he said, looking up from the fire over which he had been sitting.

'I think so; possibly four. I have rented the whole shooting from Arthur Branscombe, and he is going to board me in the house. I am not going to hunt, and I shall job such carriage-horses as I want from him.'

'Have you hired Mr. George Branscombe as coachman?' said Cross, determined to give George a *quid pro quo*.

'I have not done that,' said Struan.

'Lucky for you,' said Cross, 'or your neck would be in as much danger as his own.'

'There is more hemp ready for you than there is for me,' said George, and thought that he had said a fine thing, but

he saw that Struan was angry. Cross
replied,

'This house would be tolerable but for
you, sir. Mr. Struan, I fear that my friend
Arthur has got a good bargain out of you.
There is not very much game here. Do you
take the venison?'

'No, I never thought of that,' said Struan.
'I wish you would speak about that for me.
Ask Arthur Branscombe to let me have five
bucks in the year: I shall be very much
obliged to you if you will.'

'I will see my friend on the matter,'
said Cross; 'but he is not easy to deal
with. In the meantime, here he is listening
to us.'

Arthur had certainly come in unob-
served, save by George. His detection by
Cross and Struan rendered him silent for a
time; and then he spoke:

'You can have the deer, body and bones, if you have a mind to it. They are no use to me, or to anyone else. I should say that they were a cursed plague. They eat more than they are worth, in my opinion. But we need not talk about that now: there is something odd in the house, and I can't make it out.'

'Something odd?' said Cross.

'I fancy that it is murder,' said Arthur. 'But I do not know anything about it, and so I decline committing myself. There is the very deuce of a lot of blood down in the wine-cellars.'

As no one but Arthur ever went there, it became obvious that Arthur had either cut his throat or his finger. A committee of the whole house having proceeded there, it was discovered that there was no blood at all; but everyone saw that for some occult reason

Arthur had told a lie peculiarly clumsy even for him.

Still there was a motive in everything he did, and he left three such extremely sharp people as his brother George, Struan, and Cross to puzzle their brains hopelessly as to his motive in this case. Neither of the three, thinking separately, could make anything of the matter.

Just before bedtime, when the butler brought in the candles, they were still further puzzled. He announced that Gabriel, the young footman, had been missing all day, and that no traces had been found of him anywhere. He asked leave, therefore, to shut up the house, which Arthur gave with singular promptitude.

George, as soon as the house was quiet, went to Struan's bedroom as by appointment.

The conversation was begun rapidly by Struan.

'What do you make of this, George Branscombe?' he said.

'I'll be hanged if I know,' said George. 'I tell you the truth, Mr. Struan: it is obvious that Gabriel has hooked it.'

'Hooked what?' said Struan, puzzled.

'*It*, you know,' said George, in explanation—'vampoosed, vamosed the ranche, mizzled, stampeded, or, to be more explicit, padded his hoof.'

'Do you mean that he has gone away?' said Struan, rather amused.

'Well, if you like to use a circumlocution like that, I do mean so. And he has not only vampoosed, but Arthur is in it.'

'Why should he go away?'

'He is not safe about Cross, I suppose.

Cross has insured his life for a thousand pounds, and holds the policy.'

'The mischief! You never told me this before.'

'What time have I had to tell you, my dear sir? Be just.'

'You will find me scrupulously so. Is there anything else which you have concealed from me?'

'I don't think so,' said George. 'I can't remember everything at once.'

'Very good. You think that your brother Arthur knows of this disappearance?'

'I think so. He seldom lies except about horses or money. And even on those points he generally leaves it to me; for I have ten times his brains, and he knows it. He would never have made such an ass of himself as he did to-night unless he wanted to hoodwink the whole lot of us. And a nice mess he has made of it. But he has never really trusted me as a brother should, since I sold his horse and spent the money.'

George departed; and Struan, getting into bed, said,

'There is honesty about that man's rascality; and the curious thing is that the man is not dissipated, or in the ordinary sense of the word immoral. He is an excellent card to play against Cross.'

CHAPTER VIII.

AWAKENED MEMORIES.

No room could possibly have been a more comfortable refuge from the wildest of wild English weather than was the parlour at Grange Garden. Mrs. Lionel Branscombe found it to be so as she came in out of the weather at six o'clock one night, and casting the snow off her cloak exclaimed to Lady Alice and Lady Madeleine, 'My dear souls, you must have thought that I was lost.'

Lady Madeleine took her cloak, but the more practical Lady Alice looked at her shoes. 'Why,' she said, 'your shoes are soaked through and through; and you would have kept them on if it had not been for me. You have been to the mountain again, for there is peat as well as snow on them. Don't deny it.'

'I do not deny it,' said Edith quietly. 'I *have* been to the mountain.'

'Do you bring us any news, my dear?' said Lady Madeleine.

The answer came in a sudden burst of tears. 'Yes,' she said, 'the poor little child is dead. It stretched out its little hands, and it put up its little chin, and then its little body shook all over, and I thought that it had gone to sleep; but it was dead.'

There was silence in the room for a few moments. It was broken by Edith :

'That was the way my child died, but I was not by. I will try to forget it.'

'Do not forget it for one instant,' said Lady Alice. 'It will do you an immense deal of good to remember it, my dear. And so the little thing is dead, is it?'

'Yes, dead,' said Edith.

'I will have masses said for its soul,' said Lady Madeleine. 'I don't ask you, Alice, to put the sum down in the day-book; but you owe me sixteen shillings, and you won't begrudge *that?*'

'Not I,' said Lady Alice. 'I will willingly give five pounds in masses for the child's soul. I don't think that they will be any good, because I believe that the child is safe with its God, and can't be meddled with. Still, if you and Edith like it reckon upon me. I'm a Catholic, not a *Roman* Catholic.'

Having lived together so long, Lady Madeleine Howard was perfectly aware that

it would be idle to argue with Lady Alice
Browne. She only said, therefore,

'We are expecting some people to
supper, Edith. Mr. Wotherston is one,
whom you have met once or twice; and
Mr. Struan whom you have not met before.'

'Struan,' she said; 'oh I remember
Struan quite well. Why, he was Lionel's
bosom friend. Is he coming here to-
night?'

'Yes, my dear. Have you any objection to meet him?'

'I? None in the least; I always liked
him. By-the-bye, I got a letter from him
the other day telling me that he had returned from New Zealand. I shall only be
too happy to see him.'

'He will be here in ten minutes, then,'
said Lady Alice.

The room was very dark by the time

that Wotherston and Struan arrived; but it
was gradually lit up by George Barton, the
younger brother of Gabriel at Pollington.

Wotherston naturally spoke to Edith,
and then Struan came towards her in the
dim light.

'I need hardly introduce myself, Mrs.
Branscombe,' he said; 'you and I are very
old friends.'

'Very old indeed,' she said, giving him
her hand. 'should you have recognised
me?'

'Anywhere.'

'Well, I should not have recognised
you, Mr. Struan,' she answered with a
laugh.

'No?'

'Not for an instant,' she said; 'and
your beard puzzled me; yet you were
always so very like——'

' Like whom ? '

' Like my husband Lionel,' she said, after a pause. ' The likeness was always a singular one : it always puzzled me.'

' Did you ever dream of any reason for that likeness, Mrs. Branscombe ? '

' I never did.'

' What have you ever heard of me ? '

' That you were a young gentleman of good means, high character, and were a very close friend of my husband Lionel.'

' Are you inclined to trust me, Mrs. Branscombe ? ' he said.

' Most fully, I am sure,' she replied ; ' the more so as I recognise your voice now. It recalls me to the time when I was fool enough to suppose that there could be any happiness in this world. You were my husband's friend at Florence. Give me your hand again in remembrance of that day.'

Struan put his hand in hers.

'Madame,' he said, 'may I tell you a secret?'

'Certainly,' she replied.

'Struan, the man you know and whom you recognise, was the illegitimate brother of Lionel Branscombe.'

'I understand,' she said. 'I can feel for you, Mr. Struan. Pray tell me how you liked New Zealand, and a great deal about yourself. I, as I suppose you know, have spent the most of my time in a convent; and I shall go back again very likely, some day or another.'

'I trust you will not do that,' said Struan.

'Oh! I think I shall,' said Edith.

'I will not pursue that subject now, Mrs. Branscombe,' said Struan. 'I wish you to understand that the present Struan was

Lionel's brother; that the present Struan asks you to tell him, for his brother's sake, the whole truth of the quarrel which parted them.'

'I cannot tell, Mr. Struan,' she said; ' you come upon me too suddenly. Many had to do with it; and there were such dreadful things. The Archbishop knows all about it, and he could tell. They said that Lionel killed my child because he was jealous of my cousin. And that was so utterly unlike Lionel. Lionel a murderer! and the murderer of his own child! Yet they said he was.'

'Did you hate Lionel, Mrs. Branscombe?'

'I loved him,' she said hurriedly, 'and I love the memory of him still. I never loved any other man. The memory of him is still so dear that I can sit and talk to you, his brother, for the mere sake of the sound of your voice.'

'One question more, madam, for I shall see your husband and my brother soon. Was there ever any engagement of marriage between you and Dr. Cross?'

'I never held any words save those of civility towards any man save my husband,' she said. 'Dr. Cross? Which of them was that? I hardly remember him. Heavens —yes, I do. *Is he dead?*'

'No,' said Struan, 'he is alive.'

'Look here,' she said, taking Struan's hand again in hers, 'I ask you as my husband's own brother to beware of that man. I could tell things to my husband which I could not to you. The man terrified me, and yet I liked him to some extent. Are you a man of the world, Mr. Struan?'

'Yes.'

'Then you can possibly guess what power an unscrupulous man like Cross may have over a girl who has come from a convent, and is frightened at everything. He got such power over me. Now I remember the man, I hate the sound of his name. I think, whenever I do think of it, that he was at the bottom of everything.'

'Do you love Lionel still, Mrs. Branscombe?' said Struan.

'I love the memory of my dear husband,' she said.

'If he came to you and made his story good,' said Struan, 'would you hear him?'

'Save me from that, Mr. Struan, if you love your brother. I could not face Lionel. All has gone wrong from beginning to end. We have been parted—possibly by a foolish mistake, concerted by scoundrels—so long,

that we had better remain apart. These
good ladies here tell me that there are some
designs against his freedom. You will, I am
sure, see that nothing of the kind happens.
My poor Lionel! he would fret his life away.
But now good-bye Mr. Struan. I have talked
too much and too long.'

'May I come again?' said Struan.

'As often as you like,' she said. 'But do
not talk about *him*: that is all over.'

CHAPTER IX.

A SHELL EXPLODES IN THE GRANGE.

ADVANCED Irish patriots say that the Irish potato famine could only have occurred under English rule. That is scarcely fair, because we solemnly warned them against the exclusive cultivation of that root. Lady Alice Browne, however, though generally a reasonable woman, was unreasonably patriotic (on the Protestant or Ulster side) when she began to superintend the digging up of her potatoes. There were a great many diseased, and this Lady Alice attributed openly to the Popish incantations of Lady Madeleine Howard.

Now all that Lady Madeleine had ever done was to erect the most innocent little shrine at the other end of the trout pond, and catch lumbago by saying her prayers there instead of in her bedroom. Lady Alice had to rub mustard into her shoulders, and gave her a good slap when she had finished. She had seen shrines enough abroad, on every hillside, but she strongly objected to them in her garden.

Lady Alice also stepped round to the Parish doctor, and asked him if the potato disease was infectious, as her brother, Lord Cornelius, had once informed her. He said no, but gave here three preventive bottles one after the other, and charged her seven-and-sixpence. She made Lady Madeleine take one bottle, and took the other two herself. She found them induce precordial warmth and somnolency, combined to the curious symptom of irritability and thirst on being called in the morning.   The medicine had possibly something better or worse in it than their beer.

When the dealer came for the potatoes, Lady Alice did not happen to be perfectly ready for him, which made her rather 'chippy' in her temper : she soon, however, was prepared for battle, and met her natural enemy with a smile on her face.

He looked at the potatoes, and shook his head : then scratched it, and stood silent.

'Well, what is your offer, Master Tidey?' she said.

'Put a name to it yourself, my lady,' he said; 'I can't be buyer and seller too.'

'Say the word, man,' she replied.

'Your ladyship,' he said, 'if I was to offer eighteen-pence I should lose by it; but I am always ready to oblige a neighbour.'

Lady Alice's wrath was rising. 'Four shillings is the lowest I will take,' she said loftily.

'Why, my lady,' he said, ' be reasonable. Three-quarters of 'em are touched with the Irish rot.'

This national insult was too much. She gave the man a look which he did not understand, but which he never forgot, and ordered him off. She then went and unburdened her soul to Lady Madeleine.

'These base English peasants,' she remarked, 'have no hesitation in insulting an Irish gentlewoman. The Irish rot! How elegant! So the disease deliberately introduced from the Continent into that country for the ruin of it is to be laid at our doors. Oh, indeed! Quite so!'

'My dear, do you think they did it deliberately?' said Lady Madeleine.

'If you knew history as well as I did, you would know that it was a deliberate and cold-blooded act of the Man Peel, for the depopulation of Ireland.'

'Was not the ultimate effect to put him out of power?' said Lady Madeleine.

'It's all the same thing,' said Lady Alice. 'Serve him right. Dear me, here is somebody coming to call. A man in a brougham, I declare. I don't know the livery anywhere about here, and yet I seem to remember it too. He is sending in his name. Who can it possibly be?'

The mystery was solved. The man brought in a card which had the effect of an explosive shell, for on it was written—

Mr. Arthur Branscombe,

　　　　　　　　Pollington.

'Heavens!' said Lady Alice, 'who did he ask for?'

'For your ladyships.'

'Show him into the drawing-room directly,' said the decisive Lady Alice, 'and say we will be with him at once. This is wonderful. What can it mean?'

Arthur Branscombe had not been standing at the window five minutes—he had come to the conclusion that a fleam (a thing for bleeding horses) he had bought in Shrewsbury was on the whole cheap at three-and-sixpence,—when the two ladies, perfectly dressed, glided into the room; and Lady Alice, pointing to a seat, said, 'To what are we indebted for this honour?'

Here was a pretty beginning. Arthur had calculated on their saying, 'How do you do?' and now here they had gone and said something else. He remembered that his father had once told him that you never could reckon on a woman five minutes to-

gether; and during the time he was cogi-
tating on the singular shrewdness of the
Governor, he remained staring at the two
ladies with no expression on his face, and
perfectly silent.

Being a man of resource, however, he
bethought him of giving the answer which
he had originally composed as being better
than nothing.   He therefore said, ultimately,
'Much the same as usual, thank you; but
we all get older.'

'I am sure I do,' said Lady Alice, anxious
to conciliate him.   'If you complain of age,
Mr. Branscombe, what should I do?   I remember you a little boy.'

'I was an awful little blackguard, wasn't
I?   The Governor always said I was, and
you could always trust the Governor.'

'Well, you were a sad pickle, Mr. Branscombe,' said Lady Alice, laughing heartily at

the utter simplicity of the man. 'I was one myself—as bad as ever you were in some ways. But we don't meet now to confess old misdemeanours, do we?'

'No,' said Arthur, 'I wanted to ask you some questions about my brother Lionel, who lived here with you for some years.'

'Who sent you?' said Lady Alice.

'I came of my own free will,' said Arthur. 'Neither Struan nor Cross knew about this journey; and I hope that you will not mention it to either of them.'

'Are we likely to see them?'

'All kinds of unlikely things happen,' said Arthur. 'My brother George swindled me out of a hundred and eighty pounds about a horse of mine, and spent the money, and the other day he paid ten pounds of it back again. Now that was very honest.'

'We'll consider ourselves in your exclusive confidence, Mr. Branscombe; we shall never say a word.'

'Then I wish to ask you, did you consider Lionel mad when he was here?'

'Assuredly not: dismiss the idea from your mind at once. His happiness was wrecked for a time, but his reason was never for an instant clouded. All the splendid political action of Mr. Wotherston was, I may say, dictated by him while he was in seclusion here. Lionel has only to appear before the world again to make the whole charge unutterably ridiculous.'

'Then if Lionel has only to show and put things square, why don't he?'

That such a hopeless oaf as Arthur Branscombe should make such a singularly shrewd remark was a fact which utterly took away Lady Alice's breath; but her true Irish

heart was ready for the best lumbering
Saxon of them all.

'There were other circumstances con-
nected with Lionel's disappearance from the
world,' she said, ' which still might make it
painful for him to return to it.'

'You mean,' said Arthur, ' the suspicious
death of his child, and his quarrel with his
wife ? '

' Exactly.'

' Well, I cannot help him there ; but this
I will promise, he shall not be annoyed by
this scheme of locking him up. My brother
George and I were both in it at one time,
but now we are both out of it. What you
have said has made me resolute that it shan't
be done. I have promised that before to a
certain friend of mine, and now I mean to
keep my promise ; only I wanted to see you
two ladies before I kept it.'

This amazing piece of morality rather amused Lady Alice, while it utterly horrified Lady Madeleine: neither interrupted, because they saw that he was going on.

'I want to say something more. I had a little sister, Clara—I am afraid I was a great brute to her when she was young; now Lionel petted her, and was good to her. Now I am told that when Lionel was ruined she stuck by him when I deserted him, and behaved like a thundering—I mean in a really splendid and grateful way. Is that true?'

'*That* it is,' said Lady Madeleine, speaking for the first time with such astounding and unexpected emphasis that Arthur's wits went wool-gathering, and he looked at her as he would have done at a horse down, or a man in a fit.

'I am glad to hear it is true,' he said,

when it was in his opinion safe to go on. 'I
am very glad of that. My experience of
women is—well, you know—unfortunate.
I am bound to say that my mother led my
father a considerable life of it ; and—I have
not been lucky. Still, when a woman does
come out, you know, like you two ladies and
Clara, I am bound as a man to applaud them.
I have communicated with Clara as her
trustee often. I should immensely like to
show her in some tangible form that I do
really love the little lass after all. What can
I do?'

'Let me tell her *that*,' said Lady Alice,
'and it will be more precious to her than a
suit of diamonds.'

'No really! no really!' said Arthur
Branscombe. 'Poor little Clara!'

And there was silence in the room, which
was not quickly broken—for the two old

ladies felt that Arthur might have been a different man under different auspices; nay, that he might still be a different man; and they both in their different ways were thinking of the matter.

> And then a voice from out the farthest slope
> Cried to the summit, ' Is there any hope ? '
> Whereto an answer pealed from that high land,
> But in a voice no man could understand.

CHAPTER X.

THEY felt that the conversation was finished ; however the laws of hospitality were to be respected ; and they begged Arthur Branscombe to stay and have lunch with them. They pressed him rather eagerly to do so, for, oddly enough, they both began to like him.

'Thank you,' he said, 'I think I will stay. You see that I very seldom get any ladies' society, and that is hard on me, because I *was* born a gentleman. I will stay, if you please ; and my young man—I

will just step out, and send him to the
public-house for an hour.'

'You must not do that,' said Lady Alice,
who now observed that Arthur's brougham
had been waiting all this time. 'Have him
into our kitchen, and let him put your horse
up. By-the-by, I don't think that we *can*
put a horse up; it will be better if you will
let our servant step out and see to him. I
will give orders.'

So the young man escaped their hospitality, and Arthur was left alone with Lady
Madeleine.

'I should like,' he said, 'to give Clara
something to remember me by; but Lady
Alice thinks that my words would be
sufficient. You do not want a carriage
horse, do you, Lady Madeleine?'

'No, we keep no carriage.'

'If you fell in with anyone who did,

you might mention that I had several on hand.'

'Yes, I could do so; but we see no one.'

'You have not seen such a thing as a stray footman about, have you?' said Arthur.

Lady Madeleine, not quite hearing him, rose, and cast her eye over the carpet. 'No,' she replied, fancying that he referred to some new object of male attire or adornment, 'I really have not: have you dropped one?'

'Why, yes,' said Arthur,—'I mean Gabriel Barton. He is gone, and I thought he would have come here.'

'Gabriel Barton!' said Lady Madeleine. 'No; he has not come here.'

'Very well. I take your word as a gentleman—I mean as a lady—that he has not. If he has, keep him here. I say that to you earnestly before Lady Alice comes back. Tell her after I am gone ; but don't make me tell her, because I am afraid of her. She is down on you like my mother used to be ; but then the Governor was just as much down on her ; and when both the man and the woman come down on one another together, there's a row. And in a row with *her* I should have the worst of it. Only I tell you, if Gabriel Barton comes here, keep him here—that's all.'

The lunch passed over very well. Arthur was as agreeable as he could be. A good farmer and stockbreeder, he had much to tell the two ladies which they, with their habits of seclusion, did not know. When his brougham came up at the appointed hour, they were almost sorry to part with him, and asked him what train he was going to catch.

'Oh,' he said, 'I did not come by train. I drove all the way, doing business. My brother George drove. That is my brother George on the box (he calls it bench) now.'

'But your brother in livery, Arthur Branscombe!' said Lady Alice.

'He chose to do it. He wanted some tips about the Shrewsbury races,' said Arthur. '*I* let him, of course. Don't you see, he could get into the society of grooms by doing so.'

'But for the sake of old family connexions let him come in,' said Lady Madeleine.

'You'd better not,' said Arthur. 'He would be mad with me if he knew I had told you about it. And he does not like the society of ladies like yourselves ; he says they bore him : I did not till I met you. Ladies, in saying good-bye, I do earnestly hope that you will think the best of me— and of George. Ladies, as far as I am concerned not a hair of Lionel's head shall be

touched ; but I cannot perform impossi-
bilities. Remember me kindly to my poor
little Clara. Good-bye.' And so he went.

'There's a good man spoilt by a bad
education,' said Lady Madeleine.

'I'm not sure he is spoilt yet,' said Lady
Alice. 'There's Irish blood in that man's
veins as sure as you are born. No man but
an Irishman could have kept his heart in the
right place so long under the lowering influence of the Saxon tyranny.'

Lady Madeleine did not say anything.
They saw Arthur get into his brougham and
heard him say to George (who in livery
looked his part every inch) 'Shrewsbury ; '
and then they saw him driven rapidly away
behind a horse which they calculated as
being worth twice as much as any one of
Wotherston's.

When they were on a level and lonely

road, Arthur put his head out of the front window of the brougham, and with his chin against George's elbow discoursed familiarly.

'What will he take for that black colt?' said Arthur.

'Couldn't get him below eighty.'

'He be ——' We were very nearly committing an indiscretion.

'I'd have him, though,' said George.

'Would you now, brother?' said Arthur; 'then have him we will. You are a good buyer: that will be six pounds for you. Did you hear anything of Gabriel?'

'Not a word. He has not been near the place.'

'It is a queer thing,' said Arthur.

'*I* thought you were in it,' said George, 'and I told Struan so. Did you tell him to go away?'

'Yes.'

'Why did you do so?'

'I don't remember,' said Arthur,—a
reply that made George whip the horse
suddenly, which had the effect of knocking
Arthur's hat off into the road, so they had
to stop and pick it up. Arthur stood in the
road mournfully looking at it and wiping
it with his pocket-handkerchief. George
thought he would have been angry, but he
was only melancholy.

'I shall have to get a new one,' he said;
'eighteen and six; I could never go to
sessions in this hat now, you know. I must
have a new one.'

'I'll tell you what you do,' said George;
'get a new one on tick at Lincoln and
Bennet's; they'll let *you* have one—(they
wouldn't me I know). You'll save five per
cent. interest in reality. And then you
keep that one for going to sales: they

never run a man up hard who has got a
bad hat.'

Arthur let himself into his brougham
under the impression that George was no
fool, and determined that he would *not*
deduct a new hat out of George's next commission. He then settled himself quietly in
his carriage, and taking out his stud book,
condemned himself as a fool for not having
succeeded in cheating a horse-dealer at
Church Stretton.

Arthur Branscombe's moments of weakness were extremely rare. Had his brother
George known what had passed in the
Grange with the two old ladies, he would
not have envied the next man who had to
make a bargain with Arthur.

CHAPTER XI.

STRUAN AND CROSS HAVE A FEW WORDS.

STRUAN stayed continually at Pollington, to Cross's immense though silent annoyance, for he had frequently to be away at his practice very much, and he rather distrusted the growing influence which Struan was gaining over Arthur. Yet he disliked to move in the matter in any way, for after all Arthur was a man who would think a year before altering his will, and the money which Struan paid to Arthur for such things as he bought, and they were many, went two-thirds of it into his pocket at Arthur's death

He was disturbed at the disappearance

of the young footman, Gabriel. It was true,
as George had told Struan, that he had
insured the young man's life for a thousand
pounds a few years previously, when he was
not so certain of his position as he was now,
and had the policy assigned to him in
gratitude for recovery from an illness which
he had created, and which he had also
cured by the simple plan of withdrawing the
cause of it. Now the young man was not
to be found, and no cause of his disappearance could be discovered. Suspicions might
arise against himself, he argued; because
that fellow George knew of the insurance,
for George had once mentioned the fact
casually to him. His character was not
very high in some quarters: questions might
be asked if he claimed the money : it would
be better never to claim it: he was per-
plexed and worried about the matter, and

that perplexity was getting extremely dangerous to Arthur Branscombe.

Cross never had the remotest idea that Struan and George were hand in glove against him, that every movement of his was watched, and that George was bought over by Struan. He never thought about it; if he had, he would have considered that if George had been a secret enemy, he would have been more civil. Watched he was though.

George said to Struan one night in the latter's bedroom, 'It's as bad as having a dead corpse walking about the house at all hours as to have that man. I am afraid to eat my dinner.'

'But we can't move yet.'

'We shall all be murdered if we do not soon,' said George. 'What do you make of Gabriel's disappearance?'

'I am puzzled.'

'So is Arthur. He did send him away. Why has he not turned up at the Grange?'

That question was solved in a singular manner. Arthur one morning took Struan to show him some rare old jewels; he tried to turn the key of the casket, but the key would not turn; in contending with the lock the lid was found to be loose behind; an instant's examination showed that the hinges had been filed away: the casket was open and the jewels gone. Here was the secret of Gabriel's not being found.

Struan found time pass not at all unpleasantly at Pollington: the guest who brings not only good society but money is pretty sure to be welcome anywhere. The brothers behaved themselves before him as to some extent they used to before Cross; but Struan's influence was altogether, after a little time, different from Cross's. They

were both a little afraid of this man; and
not to be too particular, he had bought
them both; yet they liked him, and would
put themselves out of the way to do him
small services (unpaid for). There was a
marked increase of gentleness in Arthur's
manner, after their expedition to the
Grange Garden, which George was glad to
see, though he was slightly puzzled by it, as
he had only told Struan what he knew,
which was not much, for Arthur had told
him nothing about the details of his interview
with the two old ladies. If he had, he considered that George would have thought
him soft, and ' come down on him.'

Cross came and went, but Struan stayed.
George saw that there would be a battle-
royal between them some day, but it was
long delayed, and when it came off he was
not *officially* present.

Struan went shooting one morning, and
when he came back found George and
Arthur in the stables, and Cross reading in
the dining-room. He stepped up to him and
said,

'Dr. Cross, will you step up to my
room?—the coast is clear, and we can have
it out now without seconds.'

Cross was taken aback : he did not
expect the first move to come from the
enemy like this; but he was safe, so he said,

'Certainly.'

They went together to Struan's room.
They sat fronting one another, and Struan
began by saying,

'Dr. Cross, you insured the life of
this young man Gabriel who has disappeared?'

'Exactly,' said Cross, promptly. 'And
raised money on the policy, with Count

Burstenberg and Sir James Bowers as securities.'

'Thank you,' said Struan. 'I did not know as much as *that* before. I am deeply obliged to you.'

Cross had made a blunder, but Struan had made a worse one: he had let Cross see that he had made it. Struan had been wanting to identify Burstenberg, and now Cross had enabled him to do so. Cross would warn Burstenberg now, and the longest purse must win. Neither of them ever calculated, however, on Burstenberg's having become religious and telling the truth. The great city merchant, however, *was* the ex-homœopathic doctor.

'I want to know, Dr. Cross, what has become of the young man Gabriel Barton.'

'You are exactly in my situation,' said Cross. 'I am not a rich man, as all the

world knows. I have borrowed money on
that young man's life, and I don't know
where he is. I can't prove his death, and
until I do so the policy is of no value to me.
I must either drop it, and let my friends in
for the money—a thing which I cannot
afford to do—or go on paying the policies
on his life. I wish *I* knew where the man
was.'

'Yes, your case is obviously strong there.
You will never hear much of him. The
jewels he stole were of great value, were
they not?'

'No, twopenny things likely to attract
the eye of a boy.'

'I see,' said Struan. 'May I ask you
another thing : you remember Lionel Branscombe ?'

'Perfectly. You and I talked about
him some time ago'—and the Doctor con-

tinued looking him straight in the face. 'I
now know you to be his illegitimate brother.'

'How the deuce did you find that out?'
said Struan, fairly amazed and taken aback.

'Who was present at that tea-drinking
at the Grange Garden, Mr. Struan? I will
go through all the people for you: Lady
Alice, Lady Madeleine, Wotherston, Clara,
and yourself. Was there no one else?'

'Devil a soul except the devil himself,'
said Struan. 'Were *you* there, or was it the
mysterious Gabriel?'

'Neither,' said Cross, rising to his feet.
'I have information such as you never can
gain. I am everywhere. It is vain to
contend with *me*, Robert Struan.'

'I see that,' said Struan, after a pause.
'But I should like to plead for my poor
brother Lionel.'

'On your knees are you, Struan? Well,

I will tell you the truth : you have irritated
me, and I will speak out. That brother of
yours, that Lionel, took from me the only
woman I ever cared for, and I'll hunt him
down.'

'You mean Mrs. Lionel?'

'I mean Mrs. Lionel.'

'She and you went astray, I doubt.'

'You are a liar, sir,' said Cross. 'She
was a saint who even might have saved such
a sinner as myself.'

'But her Polish cousin?'

'Her favourite cousin! Well, he was
not innocent as she was. He was a great
scoundrel, and Lionel did right to shoot him.
Had he not been so, Burstenberg and I should
never—— But I am getting warm. I hope
I have not said anything to offend you.'

'You have called me a liar,' said Struan
quietly.

'Then I humbly apologise,' said Cross.
'Pray think no more about it.'

'I will not.   But about my brother
again.   Are you determined to hunt him
down?'

'I am determined to do so, sir.   I find
that he is antagonistic to me.   I allow no
person to hold that position for long.   I
have fresh information about him, and I will
have him arraigned on a charge of murder.
You are in communication with him, and
you may tell him that.'

'But how would Arthur like it?' said
Struan.

'It is a matter of indifference to me,'
said Cross.   So he rose and left the room,
and was seen airing himself on the lawn,
from the window.

In a few minutes after another door
opened, and George came in.

'Why, what a row you two have been making,' he said. 'I have been listening to every word of it.'

'Are you sure you have, and could remember it?' said Struan.

'I'd swear to that,' said George. 'He wants to hunt down Lionel; and, all said and done, Lionel was a devilish sight the best of the whole lot of us. And so you are our brother after all? I remember now about the boy called Struan—you, you know: there was a row about the Governor acknowledging the thing; and so I like the way you stick up for Lionel—be hanged if I don't; and Lionel was not a bad chap, as far as I knew him. A pretty little beggar he was; if I had a pretty little fellow like that round me, I'd be shot if I wouldn't try to do my duty by him, and take him to church, and all that sort of thing, you know.'

'And to the betting-ring also,' said Struan.

'The breed of horses must be kept up,' said George. 'If you can't do it without the weediest, neediest set of scamps in the way of betting men in God's creation, you must do it with. I've been ordered off the Heath, so I ought to know.'

'Sit here with me an hour,' said Struan, 'and let me tell you about our brother Lionel.' And George sat with him as required.

CHAPTER XII.

A MIDNIGHT MEETING.

THERE was a time when Arthur Branscombe used very frequently to go to bed in his boots. This time was long past; he now was very particular about his way of going to bed. He had no valet; not even the mysteriously departed Gabriel was allowed in his bedroom, because all the petty cash of the house was under his bed. He first of all counted his money, locked it up, locked his door, then took off his boots and put them under his bed : because he argued

M 2

that no one but a commercial traveller ever
put his boots outside the door.   On one
occasion, at the last moment, Arthur put the
lighted candle under the bed, and blew out
his boots; this, he pointed out to George,
who assisted in extinguishing the conflagra-
tion, came of attending to details after going
through your accounts for two hours.   After
taking off his boots, he used to sit on his
bed, and piously meditate on the events of
the day : if nobody had cheated him, or if
he had cheated anybody, he used to undress
and get into bed at peace with his fellow-
creatures, and sleep calmly : if, on the other
hand, he felt that he had not done himself
justice, and improved each shining hour to
his best advantage, he used to go through
a course of self-examination and abasement,
repenting, and determining on future amend-
ment, — for the devil has *his* litanies as

well as heaven, and they are more easily
learnt under the tuition of his arch-priest
Self.

To-night his meditations were extremely
disturbed. He had not even counted his
money, though he had locked the door.
He tried to think of what he had been
doing, but whenever he did so he always
found himself thinking about his father.
Now I have before said that Arthur's father,
or 'Governor,' was to a large extent an
ideal of his own creation. Old Branscombe had been very little less disagreeable
to Arthur than he had been to everybody
else, himself included, but Arthur had by
degrees become to believe in him as a demi-
god—a fact which showed a power of imagi-
nation where it was least to be expected,
and an amiable trait in a character in which
there were few to spare. His mind to-night

persistently ran on the Governor, and he could not get rid of him.

He started from the bed on which he was sitting, and dashed to the case where he kept his revolver, for someone had touched him on the shoulder. He was as brave as a lion, but he was completely terrified. In his locked chamber in the dead of night a hand had been laid on his shoulder. The bravest man would quail under such circumstances: with his pistol in his hand, however, he cared neither for man nor devil; and he turned upon his midnight foe with confidence.

'Don't shoot *me*, Arthur,' said George, laughing. 'I am not the right man.'

Arthur immediately put away his pistol, undressed himself, and got into bed. 'Now,' he said from his pillow, 'perhaps you will inform me how the devil you got here.'

'Through that door,' said George, sitting down on the bed and pointing to a door in the wainscot.

'But it has been locked up ever since I slept in this room, and the key is in my bureau downstairs. I saw it yesterday.'

'Most likely; but did you never hear of a key being abstracted just so long as to get it cast in wax, and another made? Because that is what has been done.' ·

'By whom?'

'By Cross.'

'But why?—what can he want in my bedroom?'

'To send you to sleep for ever, you idiot. Have you not given him everything, and told him so?'

'He would never do that; he saved my life.'

'Until you made this will. Now I am

getting uneasy about the matter. I have
my ideas that you are to go. Both Gabriel
and I have suspected it a long time; and
if you remember that time when Cross
drugged you, and made out you were
drunk——'

'Drugged me!'

'Of course,' said George, impatiently.
'Do you ever get drunk? I should make
better bargains out of you if you did. On that
occasion I slept with you, and Gabriel slept
across the door. Cross did that in hopes that
you would not lock the door, and he might
have a rummage at your papers, which he
knew you kept here. Good heavens! I have
been up to every move in every game for
fifteen years, and do you think that I did
not see *that?* Cross saw that he was suspected, and we took uncommon good care
of ourselves, but he bowled us out by think-

ing of having a key made to that old door.
I only found that out ten days ago, and I
played the same trick on him that he did on
you—got a cast of his key, and had it made
by Ninian Chaloner: he remarked to me that
Dr. Cross had had such a key made by him
before. You are a very heavy sleeper, and
Cross has been in your room three times
during his last visit. Do you wish this to
continue, or would you rather prove the
fact ?'

'I feel it hard to believe anything
against Cross,' said Arthur.

'And on my testimony, you would add,'
said George. 'Will you believe your own
eyes? I believe that I could get him to
come here any night.'

Arthur hesitated. He believed Cross
capable of being false to anyone except
himself.

'Why are you so anxious about my life, George?' he said; 'you'd be better off without me.'

'Hang it, a man's not a dog, and a fellow's brother *is* his brother. You have not always been kind to me, but you are the only fellow I care about except Struan. Besides, I hate Cross.'

'Are you sure?' Arthur was going on, when George suddenly blew out the candle, and saying emphatically to his brother 'Go to sleep,—do you hear, you fool?—he is coming,' ensconced himself behind the sofa.

Arthur went fast asleep with a rapidity unusual to him. He tried to snore, but being unaccustomed to do so when awake made what would have been called by a connoisseur rather a mess of it. Asleep he was, however, in two seconds. An intensely jealous and suspicious man naturally and by

habit, George had said enough to keep him
on the *qui vive* for the next ten years.
George hoped in time to destroy Cross's influence with him : Cross himself, that mighty
genius of plotters, did his work for him
in ten minutes.

The door by which George had entered
was stealthily unlocked, and Cross stood in
the room in the darkness.   Arthur slept
violently, but gave up the snoring as a bad
job.   George said to himself behind the
sofa, 'You come the gentle chloroform
business, my lad, and I am ready for you.'

But Dr. Cross did not 'come' that part
of his art.   When he had assured himself
that Arthur Branscombe was asleep heavily,
he showed a light from a policeman's lant-
horn, at which George said to himself,
'Now if he sees my legs, there will be a
blow-up before I wish it.   I wonder what

he wants. It is not murder; he wouldn't do that yet. I wonder what it is.'

Arthur's dressing-case, apparently. 'Murder it is,' said George. ' Oh, why isn't there anyone here to bet ? I'd give six to four on the event in poneys.'

Dr. Cross went to the dressing-case, and removed one of the bottles, which he put in his pocket. 'Then,' said George to himself, ' this is not the prussic acid dodge after all : I should have lost my money. However, Arthur is awake now.'

He was awake in more senses than one, for a voice came from his bed which said sleepily, ' Is that you, Cross ? '

' Idiot ! ' said George to himself : in which remark he was mistaken.

' I am so glad you are here,' said Arthur ; ' it was kind of you to come ; and I am glad I left the door unlocked, otherwise you

couldn't have got in. I am in the most awful pain.'

'Where?' said Cross eagerly.

Arthur indicated his back, and Cross
might have heard the sofa shaking with
George's suppressed laughter.

'I will put you up something which will
relieve it,' he said.

'No,' said Arthur, 'I don't want any
doctor's stuff; unlock the door, and call for
Mrs. Bradley to make a mustard poultice.'

Cross actually went to the ordinary door
and unlocked it. It is very strange how
great criminals commit themselves sometimes,
though not so often as is thought. If Cross
had believed that he was dealing with the
veriest idiot in the world, he could have
done no worse than openly unlock the door
from the inside. As it was, he was dealing
with a person he knew to be in his way

singularly shrewd and suspicious. The detail never struck him.

Mrs. Bradley was called up, however, and Arthur was attended to unprofessionally. Dr. Cross had an anxiety to see him later in the night, and did so. Arthur was sleeping quietly; but beside him, on the bed, was his handsome fox-eyed brother George, with his arm round his neck; and the language which I can command cannot tell you how enormously wide awake he was.

CHAPTER XIII.

ARTHUR ASTONISHES GEORGE.

Cross was in a great state of anxiety and annoyance. He might have put Arthur Branscombe to sleep a dozen times over, even after he had been assured of the contents of his will; but for the sake of a few pounds more of the man Struan's money he was close upon letting the whole thing out of his hands.

He had put himself in a very false position. Arthur had found him in his bedroom, and had asked him to unlock the door from the inside. Whether the blundering brute would ever remember that fact or not, Cross could not say. He sometimes remembered things which Cross had forgotten. If he ever did realise that fact, if his suspicions were once aroused, Cross knew that nothing would quiet them. Arthur was the most suspicious man he had ever known, and were his faith in him once shaken, he knew that the edifice of his fortune would come toppling down.

He had studied murder as a science, not only medically, but legally. 'Two people in a murder,' he argued, ' are pretty certain to spoil the whole thing. George suspects me, and I should have to get rid of him first ; afterwards of the lad Gabriel, whom I can't find. Then Struan hangs about most suspiciously with George, and that fellow would tell anything for money. I can't see my way. I have been a fool.'

What would he have said had he known
of the interview between Arthur and George,
—that George was behind the sofa, and that
Arthur's suspicions were not only aroused,
but confirmed,—that he had not one friend
left in the world?

He met Arthur at breakfast, not looking
very ill. Arthur received him with great
bonhomie, and told him how sorry he was to
have troubled him in the night. 'I hope to
heaven that it was not glanders,' said Arthur;
' the horses have got it down at Mill Farm,
and I know it is very catching. It takes
you in the shoulders first, you know.'

Cross wondered whether he was suspected. Arthur knew more about glanders
than he did, and was clumsily humbugging
him.

'I am going to London,' he said; ' can I
have your brougham, Arthur?'

'To be sure,' said Arthur. 'I am sorry you are going.'

'I'll drive you,' said the indiscreet George; but Cross preferred Jacob, and would not trouble George to drive him, any more than George would have troubled Cross to doctor him had he been poorly. Cross departed to the station under the guidance of Jacob, utterly baffled for the present, and terrified for the future.

'Had Arthur found him out?' he kept saying to himself as the train went on. That he could not decide, but one thing was certain, that with George and Struan at Pollington he must change his basis of operations, and what is more, act on the enemy quickly.

Who was the enemy? Arthur Branscombe, the only man who had ever loved him, and whose hand had loaded him with favours!

There are such men. They are men who worship self, and self alone, until they obey their idol implicitly. These men have sold themselves to the devil

Arthur Branscombe was, as far as his intellect went, an inferior person : I do not set him up beside his brother George for an instant ; George had more talent though less cash. Arthur Branscombe also was not a good fellow by any means ; perhaps, if he had had a different ' governor ' he might have been different. But there was a ' soft side ' in the man, as George knew well, which side the same George had very frequently cursed when it did not turn towards him and Arthur's moneybox at the same time. The parting between the ungrateful rascal Cross and Arthur was final, as Arthur thought. Cross went away in one frame of mind, Arthur remained behind in another.

George and Arthur were left alone after his departure, and George with his cunning instinct refused to speak.   The silence on Arthur's part was so long, that he lit a cigar in the breakfast room, a thing which he knew Arthur hated, and which he thought would lead to a conversation, which, if not complimentary, would assuredly break the ice.

Arthur, however, was not angry.   He took a cigar himself, but he never lit it.   He went to the window with it, and looked out into the deer park.   Then he leant his head upon the sill of the window, and after a time George saw from the motion of his shoulders that he was sobbing.

George could stand a great deal, as our readers have doubtless discovered by this time, but he could not stand this.   Cad as he was, he could not stand a crying woman *in presento*, though in his *rôle* of gambler he had made many gamblers' wives cry when he was absent. But to see a man cry, that was terrible, and of all men in creation Arthur!

He went quietly to Arthur, and said, ' I say, this won't do, you know. I can't stand this.'

Arthur confronted him quietly, almost with dignity.

' George,' he said, ' I am very sorry to have annoyed you. You have done your duty by me, and I thank you. But Cross was the only man I have cared for for some years, and I see that he has been seeking my life. This is the bitterest thing which ever happened to me.'

' I quite believe it,' said George heartily ; ' but give every man fair play. Don't condemn anyone in a hurry. Perhaps he might not have meant any harm—at least at present.'

' You saw him take a bottle from my dressing-case ? '

' Yes.'

' It has been put back this morning.   He made believe that I was not up, and went into my room while I was out at the stables. The attar of rose bottle, which was nearly empty, is now full.'

'Good heavens,' said George, 'what an escape!   But how can you cry over such a skunk as that ? '

' He is very dear to me, George.   He was a friend to me when everyone gave the pair of us up for hopeless blackguards.   I never did anything except loving-kindness to him, and he seeks my life, to get the money I left him.'

George remained silent.   He was gentleman enough for that. Arthur also remained silent for a time; then he came out with an astounding proposition.

' Did it ever strike you, George, that your interests and Cross's were identical ?— that you and Cross would both have served your own interests by putting me out of the way ?'

' Yes, I suppose we should have; but I am not one to murder my brother. I have watched your life carefully when you have been rudest to me. There have been times when I wished you were dead, but I don't wish you dead now. You are changed towards me since Struan came here.'

' I will remain so,' said Arthur quietly. ' I want to say one thing more to you George: about Lionel.'

George visibly started.

' Cross is going to annoy him. Now,

although I will never touch Cross, I will not
have Lionel annoyed. You will help me in
this ?'

'Most surely,' said George.

'You see, George,' continued Arthur,
'that my poor dear friend Cross has been
indiscreet; he has filled my little attar of
rose bottle with prussic acid. I poisoned
a cat with one-tenth of it this morning. You
and I can swear that we saw him take the
bottle, and so his life is in our hands. But
I won't have him touched. We must play
off anything we know against what he tries
to do with Lionel.'

'But, Arthur,' said George, 'does he
know nothing against you ?'

'I am afraid he does,' said Arthur, 'but
I'll chance that. I don't think he will make
much of it: I must take the consequence if
he does. The time is so long ago, and his

silence would be accounted for by my will.
I don't think that the poor fellow will play
that card. If he does, you must keep house
here while I am in gaol. They won't give
me very long. But I shall be put out of the
commission of the peace, and I do like
Sessions so. It makes me feel as if I was a
gentleman. And I am sure I am a gentle
magistrate.'

Struan came in equipped for shooting.

'I think I will kill a buck to-day, if I
get near one, Arthur Branscombe,' he said.

'By all means,' said Arthur, instan-
taneously getting into the depths of confusion
by the sudden change of subject, as he
always did. 'Take him clean through the
head, sir, I pray you, for it was a wasting of
God's victuals the way you killed the last.
Your bullet was lodged between the eighth
and ninth cervicular vertebra, and Parson

Dickson as nearly as possible swallowed it —he is a hasty eater. The Scotch are barbarians, and kill their deer behind the shoulder, which might play the devil with the humbles, which the servants' hall consider venison. I'd be glad if you would allow me a haunch, at butcher's price, sir, for Lady Madeleine Howard and Lady Alice Browne.'

'I should be delighted to give you one, Mr. Branscombe.'

'No,' said Arthur, 'I would sooner buy it. I don't like to give *them*, at all events, anything which cost me nothing. You see, Mr. Struan, they were devilish kind to my little sister Clara, when I neglected her, and she needed kindness. I'll buy it if you please.'

CHAPTER XIV.

A MEETING.

WE must return to the Grange at Weston.
I regret to say that there was very sad
trouble there, and that Lady Alice Brown
could not sleep for two nights running.
She had bought a new atmospheric churn,
and she could not make it go. The butter
would not come. Now as that is known to
be the most perfect of all churns, it is
obvious that the fault was on her side. She
had bought it in consequence of an adver- •
tisement in the ' Field,' and Lady Madeleine
had suggested that she had not read up all

the details about the implement. At breakfast on the third morning of her troubles,
then, she took up the 'Field' to look for
the advertisement, and see if she was wrong :
she read it aloud, as she took her toast and
tea,—or, to be more correct, made comments
on it.

'Horse-racing—five meetings! I wish
Cromwell was at their ears : my opinion
he'd stop it soon enough. The English
have introduced it into Ireland, now—
another nail in the poor country's coffin.
My brother Cornelius won the King's Plate
at Punchestown, beating all the English
horses : 'twas we Irish invented the sport
and taught it to the English ; they never
would have had go enough in them to think
about it. A pure Scotch Colley dog 25*l*.,—
there's for you. ; and I got the finest puppy
ever was seen at Castle Browne, when I was

a girl for eighteen-pence; and Cornelius
taught him to go up a ladder, but he never
could teach him to come down again; and
when they were mending the chimney he
went up the ladder after young Dennis
Moriarty, that shot at the agent for giving
his brother, Lanty Moriarty, the four-acre
croft,—and I'd like to see the Scotch dog
that would do that. But the Scotch are the
people to draw the money,—however, they
are Protestants, with all their faults. Here's
a picture of a man's hunting breeches; it's
not decent to put such things in,—and here's
another one of a man with nothing on him
but his shirt and drawers. Here's a man
sitting astride of a saddle-tree and playing at
horses: he's a lunatic I suppose, the one
that is going to give five-and-twenty pounds
for the Scotch Colley. " Hammond and
Tanby " breeches makers,—that's not proper

again; but there's a lovely picture of their
house—wonder why everybody is selling
their houses, and it is just as bad with the
estates; living too fast I suppose.'

'For what are you searching the "Field"
so deeply, Lady Alice?' said the pleasant
voice of Edith as she came into the room.

'About the new churn, my dear,' she
said. 'And where have you been?—your
tea will be cold.'

'I have been delayed with old Mrs.
Brown,' said Edith. 'She has discovered
my religion and wants to convert me.'

'She had better convert herself, the old
trot,' said Lady Alice. 'She pretended she
was converted herself once, but that didn't
prevent her getting nearly tipsy at the
harvest-home. I am sure I hope no one
will ever go and convert Madeleine there;
we should have nothing left to quarrel about.'

'But now,' said Edith, sitting down to her breakfast, 'what are your anxieties— still about the churn?'

'Yes, bad luck to it!'

'Well, I am happy to tell you that I remember all about it : there was one at the convent.'

'You are a jewel,' said Lady Alice, and after breakfast she took her away to the dairy.

When anything of importance was impending, Lady Alice used always to raise a storm over small matters. She no more cared about the churn than she did for Farmer Joyce's pigs just now. She was extremely nervous, and so was Lady Madeleine,—the latter, instead of consoling herself by loud talking over small matters, went very silently about her household duties, leaving Lady Alice to keep Edith busy and out of the way.

That was successfully done : the battle with the churn having ended under Edith's generalship in a decided victory for Lady Alice, she was asked to come into the garden and help, which she did until nearly noon.

At that time Lady Madeleine came out and asked Edith if she would go into the drawing-room and find her work for her, for she was going to do it in the sun. Edith sped away on her task with a smiling face, while Lady Madeleine said to Lady Alice, 'God speed us!' And Lady Alice came up and gave her a great kiss.

But we must follow Edith. The passage leading to the drawing-room was very dark, but when she opened the door the brilliant flood of light from the sunlit garden dazed her. She paused for an instant, for a lady was standing at the window, with her back towards her, looking pensively at the vivid mass of flowers which stretched away to the two cedars.

'I beg your pardon,' said Edith; 'but I did not know that anyone was here.'

The lady turned and said,

'Edith, do you not remember me?'

'Good heavens! it is Clara,' said Edith, starting back.

'Yes,' said Clara advancing; 'it is I. Should you know me?'

'I know you now, but I should scarcely have known you had I met you casually. Clara, you are greatly changed.'

'I need be after what I have gone through, my dearest sister,' said Clara, embracing her. 'You must always remember how dear you are to me: the short time I spent with you was the happiest of my life. You gave me a glimpse of that

brilliant world which is now closed to both
of us for ever.'

'For me,—not for you, Clara,' said
Edith, sitting beside her, and putting her
arm round her waist. 'There is beauty
enough left here to make the world admire.'

'Beauty! Yes, there is beauty in a
ruined castle, which will never more be
bright with the preparations for a tourna-
ment. I look very old in face, and I am
older than I look in experience. I have
borne the burden and heat of the day, and
it has told upon my good looks. A few
years ago, Edith, I looked as though I were
eighty. But these good women here were
very kind to me through all my terrible
time, and you see that I am handsome
again; at least so my lover, who was faithful to me through it all—God bless him!—
tells me.'

'Clara,' said Edith, 'can you tell me about Lionel?'

'Yes,' said Clara, quietly. 'When he was driven mad by villains, his wife deserted him, but his sister stuck to him.'

This was a clumsy home-thrust on the part of Clara which she should not have made. Edith withdrew her arm and sat still; Clara set herself to tie up the thread which she had broken.

'When he was maddened by the lies of these villains, and when you were deceived, we fled together here. I do not wish to recall the terrible past; I only wish to say that this was the only refuge which we had in the world. Look out into the garden, Edith; think of him in his seclusion there for so many years, like a black hideous shadow among the flowers; think of that,

and of the terrible times which I had with
him, and forgive him.'

'I have forgiven him long ago; but he
has ceased to love me, and therefore what
does my forgiveness matter?'

'I know what you mean; you mean
that you have forgiven him religiously.
You say he ceased to love you. My
wretched task would have been easier had
he done so. You had from him a love
which you never deserved, which you were
utterly unworthy of, which never wavered,
and which exists still.'

It was extremely fortunate for Clara that
Lady Alice Browne was at the lower end of
the garden tending the flowers in front of
Lady Madeleine Howard's popish shrine,
and carefully dusting the images on it,
which she conceived theoretically to be the
abomination of desolation, but which, how-

ever, were Lady Madeleine's, and therefore
sacred in *her* eyes. Otherwise, Lady Alice
would possibly have boxed Clara's ears for
losing her temper, in an affair which required so much delicacy. Perhaps Clara
was right. She went on :

'You believed those scoundrels. *I* never
did. If I had, I should have stayed by him.
He was the first friend I ever had. When I
was a poor, miserable, despised child, in a
house such as you, Edith, can have no con-
ception of; when my brothers, Arthur and
George, did nothing but curse me, and wish
I was dead, Lionel made me his friend. If
it had not been for him and Lady Madeleine,
I should have grown up a savage like my
brothers. He saved me from the hell in
which they are living, and I did not one-half
of my duty by him when I abandoned love,
success in the world, everything to help him.

I was not brought up in a convent ; I was
brought up in an extremely disreputable
house. You *were* brought up in a convent.
I had seen the devil, and knew how to face
him ; he had been kept carefully out of your
sight, and on his first appearance you fled,.
and deserted the best and noblest of human
beings.   And after it all, that man and I
love you still.'

Edith said, after a long pause, ' I believe
him now to be utterly innocent of all that I
foolishly suspected him of. But he killed my
cousin.'

' Gallant fellow, yes,' said Clara. ' Your
cousin was one of the most fearful villains
who ever lived. We know that how Lionel
was mad because he thought that he had
shot the wrong man : we know all now. If
Lionel had shot two others, he would have
ridden the earth of two more scoundrels.

And innocent soldiers are shot every day. The law gives no redress for such wrongs as Lionel has suffered, and he was right to take the law into his own hands.'

' Do you say that he loves me still? '

' Yes! with a devotion of which you are unworthy. See him, and hear him speak.'

' I could not do that,' said Edith, after a pause. 'At least I think not, just now. I want time, Clara; I want time. You can not have the slightest idea of the fearful perplexity I am in. Clara dear, we were always good friends; let me lay my head on your shoulder, and tell you that if I were to tell Lady Madeleine or Lady Alice the truth, they would turn me out of the house.'

' Well, I have been through a great deal,' said Clara. 'I can bear anything. Can you tell me your secret? '

'I dare not tell it to my director,' she replied. 'Clara, pity me.'

'I guess your secret, and pity you,' said Clara. 'You love another man.'

'I most solemnly declare that I do not,' said Edith. 'How should I? I shall go back into the convent; it is the only place for me. Will you tell me one thing—is Lionel well?'

'He is very well.'

'But the wound—does that trouble him?'

'The wound is a dreadful one, but he does not suffer. Now I must go to the two old ladies in the garden. Shall I give your love to Lionel?'

'Yes, Clara,—my dearest, tenderest love. Tell Lionel that I cannot see him, and that I shall remain here safe in this garden until I go back to the convent for ever. Tell him

to forget me. I will pray for him in my
solitude.'

So they separated, and Clara went out
and talked to the two ladies in the garden.

The ladies were in a little trouble.
Lady Madeleine had sent an order to Munich
for a three-foot St. Joseph, and they had
sent her St. Christopher instead, and he had
been considerably chipped about the nose *in.
transitu.* They had put him up on one side
of the shrine, beyond the trout pond, however, and he was not successful; he wouldn't
stand straight, although Lady Alice put a
tile under him, and then came away to look
at the effect. Alas! a puff of wind hurled
him down, and he broke in three pieces—
Lady Alice said, with a slight want of taste,
like the pagan god Dagon in the Apocrypha.

'Well,' said Lady Alice, 'there goes six
pound ten of your money. Don't cry,

dearest. I'll write to London to Mrs. Little, and get ye a new one as good as this. Ye should have stuck to her, and not sent to the Germans for your images. I'll make ye a Christmas present of one, and give it ye in September. In my opinion all the holy saints ought to have umbrellas in the rainy English climate; in Ireland they could get on without. So now, Maddy, don't sorrow about your image; I'll get ye a better one, and give five pounds to Peter's pence (that my father's daughter should do it!) if ye won't cry. See, here is Clara come to us. Well, Clara, and how have you fared?'

'I cannot tell you one single word, Lady Alice,' said Clara. 'Nothing shall induce me to do so. I don't completely make her out. She is on her trial still; I do not know how she will turn out at all. Father Wilson has played a strange game: Heaven only knows who will win it. Now I'll talk no more. Has James been for me?'

It occurred to Lady Madeleine that the postern gate was locked. On its being opened, the Liberal member was discovered sitting on a log of fallen timber, and reading 'Vivian Grey.'

CHAPTER XV.

CROSS COMMITS HIMSELF.

Cross was a man who considered it necessary in his line of practice to ' show '—not only with a well-appointed brougham on his professional visits, but at evening parties, perfectly dressed, and also in the Park with a faultless groom behind him.

The untameable old surgeon used to wonder at what price that young man's life was insured : he would bet it was five hundred, and in that he was wrong ; it was two thousand.   But the young man had merely done what he was told, like Gabriel, and was by no means anxious about his own life. The doctor was a good master to him.

Cross knew a horse, and he knew that the majority of the people did so also. He was a keen lover of horses, and knew a sound horse when he saw one. He was also a consummate horseman, and could ride 'cattle' (and show them up well too) which timid people would not cross twice. And he never dealt; he was too clever for that. If he had put George Branscombe on one of his horses, George would have ridden the horse as well as Cross, and then have begun a deal. Cross knew better. When anyone offered to buy a horse of Cross, he shook his head, and said, '*I* can ride him, but I could not trust him to anyone else.' Consequently old Cross had among fast men the character of being very honest about horseflesh, which

George Branscombe had not,—though pos-, sibly George Branscombe was the more honest man of the two.

Things were by no means safe with Cross. He could not trust George Brans-combe any longer, and it was most necessary for him to act : how, he did not exactly see. In this wicked world he had made more enemies than friends, popular as he was, and it behoved him to look around him. It was pre-eminently necessary, as he saw, that he must murder Arthur Brans-combe before he altered his will. Perhaps if he had known that Arthur Branscombe had certainly made a will in his favour, had signed it, but had never, in his blundering way, had it witnessed, he would have acted differently.

He had ordered his horse to be ready as soon as his few and very wealthy patients

were done with. Consequently he was riding
in the Park by half-past three.

There were few handsomer or better-
mounted men there than he. He knew a
great many of a certain class of people, some
with titles, some without, but all hangers-on
of the lowest edge of the English aristocracy.
Half-way up the Row he saw a Personage
coming, and alongside this Personage, to his
astonishment, Struan, conversing eagerly with
him. Cross rode more carefully than ever,
and said, ' That fellow Struan could get in
anywhere ; I can't.' The Personage mean-
while was curling up his white moustache,
and saying to Struan, ' Look at that fellow
Cross, riding about here as if he was not
found out. Why, good Lord, that fellow
ought to be kicked out of every mess in the
army.'

Still the Personage said, ' How are you

Cross?' as they passed; and Struan said, 'How are you, Doctor?' It was enough for Cross—he was recognised. A man between the devil and the deep sea, as he was, was glad even of that.

So he rode solemnly on. The swift tramp of a horse's feet arrested beside him aroused him; he turned round, and saw that the horseman was Struan.

'Dr. Cross,' he said, 'our last interview was not a very pleasant one. For the sake of Lionel Branscombe, I am naturally most eager to be your friend. Will you come and dine with me to-day?—and excuse chambers at the Albany, for I am not settled.'

Nothing Cross would like better; it was the very thing he wanted. He accepted gladly; and riding a little way with Struan, who had a wave of the hand from the Personage, felt himself again.

If he could only gain over Struan, even for a short time! Arthur's behaviour had certainly been odd to him when he came away, but as Cross honestly said to himself, 'It may only be my conscience, after all; I'll make friends with this man, for I hold my power over Lionel Branscombe just the same, and I shall let him know it. *Bon.*'

Cross dearly liked a good dinner, and he got one. He was most brilliant, amiable, and agreeable, as usual; and Struan was the same. The conversation went on most pleasantly for a long time, and we take it up where Cross said—

'His Royal Highness looks uncommonly well.'

'Singularly so. He is scarcely changed since I went away.'

'I remember now that you were in the

army,' said Cross. 'He is like a father to all his officers, and never forgets one. Plenty of young fellows I have known have been kept out of mischief by him.'

The Personage might have said that this was singularly true, as one thing always in his mouth was, 'Take care of that fellow Cross as you would of the devil.'

'Yes, he does his duty well in every way. I wish that he had had the guidance of George Branscombe.'

'He could have done no good there, sir; not a bit. There was no stuff to work on. In my profession I have seen a few things, and I must say that I never saw an entirely depraved nature such as that of George Branscombe.'

'Are you sure, my dear Doctor, that you do not do him an injustice? I found him tractable enough.'

'With money, my dear sir, with money.'

'Yes,' said Struan, thoughtfully and slowly, 'I allow that he has had money from me. To a man of your acumen, Doctor, it is hopeless to disguise the fact that there are delicate matters in every man's life in which a certain sort of person is required as negotiator. Such a person is George Branscombe, and I have employed him.'

'I wish to heavens that you had employed me,' said Cross to himself, but went on aloud—

'You employed an extremely slippery agent, sir. I have done a good deal of that sort of work myself,—or to be more correct,' he added, rather hurriedly, 'have *seen* a good deal of it.'

'I have no doubt,' said Struan. 'There are three kinds of cigars here: would you choose?'

Cross chose, and began smoking. Struan knew, possibly from his colonial experience in countries where men smoke but seldom drink, that tobacco was more apt to open a man's mouth than wine.

'That is a curious establishment at Pollington, Mr. Struan,' began Cross; 'a very curious establishment.'

'I find it comfortable enough,' said Struan. 'The brothers are bears, but there does not seem to be much harm in them.'

'Don't you find it rather hard to get on with a cub like Arthur?' said Cross.

'No; I cannot say that I do.'

'But don't you find that their perpetual quarrels annoy you?'

'I am amused by them sometimes,' said Struan. 'They have got used to me, and appear in their native colours: they don't in fact, mind me. It appears that some time ago George sold a horse of Arthur's, and never came home until he had spent the money. Lately George paid Arthur ten pounds on account, which Arthur considers so honourable that he insists on playing off the balance at billiards, which, even supposing he loses, will take some years, because they are an excellent match at that game. Arthur firmly believes that he is treating his brother in the most liberal way by doing this, as is possibly the case; but the odd thing is that George, sharp as he is, believes in it, which amuses me intensely. Well, they are a comical pair, Dr. Cross; but as the world goes there is no great harm in them. And they are very fond of one another.'

'As fond as Cain and Abel,' said Cross. 'Until that rascal George gets hung, Arthur's life is not safe.'

'But you are hardly justified in saying that, Dr. Cross,' said Struan.

'I am perfectly justified, sir,' he replied. 'George is a hopeless and desperate man. He exists solely on his brother's bounty, which might be cut off any day. George is capable of anything, and I tremble whenever I leave Pollington, lest I should hear of Arthur's death.'

'But, my dear Doctor, don't you acknowledge that George is one of the sharpest fellows you ever met?'

'I do so, sir; he knows his interests.'

'Then,' said Struan, 'do you tell me that George as *hæres expectans* would be idiot enough to put his brother to death? Why the parish constable would arrest him on the spot as the only likely person to do such a thing.'

'Sir,' said Dr. Cross, 'I have studied

medical jurisprudence, and I know that the greatest criminals—never mind their shrewdness—are the greatest idiots.'

' I quite agree with you,' said Struan. ' But I should not have said that George was a great criminal.'

' Very good, sir. You mark the result.'

' You have been paying George considerable sums of money, have you not?' said Cross, after a pause.

' Why yes, considerable for him ; and he has done his duty very well. Is there anyone who has an interest in the death of Arthur Branscombe except himself?'

' I am afraid, one.'

' And who is he?'

' Lionel.'

' My legitimate half-brother,—I see : I, as you know, speak always in his favour.

You mean to accuse him of the murder of his child ? '

' Such is certainly my intention,' said Cross, ' the moment he reappears.'

There was a long silence, broken at last by Struan.

' Dr. Cross,' he said, ' you and I are men of the world, and no man of the world ever takes offence at what another man of the world says. In the world there is no morality.'

Dr. Cross indignantly denied that. He stood there (he was sitting down) as a monument of morality himself, and he could not hear such atrocious sentiments uttered : he had lived moral, and would die moral. He rose.

' Sit down, Doctor, and see if we cannot manage this little matter,' said Struan, taking out a large cheque-book. The Doctor instantly sat down in a state of fuming, virtuous indignation on the edge of his chair.

'You see that I don't want to have Lionel annoyed should he ever appear again in this world, which is very doubtful. If you will sign a paper which I will write out, I will give you a cheque for two hundred pounds.'

'I could not do it at the——I could not possibly think of such a thing for a moment,' said Dr. Cross. 'And I have not seen the paper.'

Struan produced it. It ran thus:

'I declare that Mr. Lionel Branscombe is entirely innocent of the charge brought against him about the murder of his child; and on receipt of two hundred pounds from Robert Struan, Esq., I undertake to abandon any future persecution of him.'

'This awaits your signature only,' said Struan.

Cross thought for a few moments, and his better angel came to his rescue.

'Sir,' he said, rising with the dignity of an honest man, 'the sum which you offer is not sufficient. I could not sign that paper under five hundred.'

'But you would do it for that,' said Struan, 'my dear Doctor? For five hundred you would absolutely say that Lionel was entirely free of all blame?'

'Most certainly I would,' said Cross; 'and it would be merely the truth.'

'The sum you ask is a large one, Doctor, and you must give me time to think about it. It may be worth my while to give it, but I don't see my way to it at this moment. I understand you that you will, if necessary, swear that Lionel was innocent for the sum named.'

'I can swear that it is the truth,

sir,' said Cross. 'When shall I see you again?'

'On Monday, I think. I must go down to Pollington, and guard Arthur.'

'I should be a better guardian than you, sir,' said Cross, putting on his top-coat. 'But I have no doubt but that we shall come to terms.'

'There is no doubt about that,' said Struan, 'for I will spend any money to prevent having Lionel annoyed.' So Cross went.

Two minutes after the oak was sported. Struan was sitting over the fire with a very nice little man, who said,

'My dear fellow, let me have a cigar and a pair of slippers, for I have new shoes on, and my corns are shooting like Sister Podagra's at Waterloo.' Whereupon Struan called out, 'Gabriel, bring my slippers, for

Father Wilson.' Whereupon Gabriel Barton brought the slippers, and Father Wilson put them on.

'We have got him now,' said Father Wilson, lighting a cigar.

'I think so,' said Struan. 'But we must be very careful.'

'We must,' said Wilson.

CHAPTER XVI.

A FAMILY GATHERING.

It may have been observed in the previous pages that the Rector of Weston has never appeared. Possibly the reason is not very far to seek: he was a High Churchman, which displeased Lady Alice, and he had of course very little in common with Lady Madeleine. The poor man was not comfortable at the Grange. However, on this occasion, he was asked to breakfast there at eleven o'clock, and he hoped that he might like it, but was very much wishing that he was safe out of it and at home again. He knew what he had to do : but he very much wished that he had not been asked to breakfast.

Clara was in her room, and Edith was helping to dress her.

'You make a beautiful bride after all, Clara,' she said. 'I was as handsome as you are once. You will never repent this step. You have kept him waiting many years.'

'And see how he has waited,' said Clara. 'Look at the man's trust, his confidence, and his diligence about public affairs through all. I am sure that I am doing right.'

'Shall you leave Lionel?' said Edith.

'I suppose so, to a certain extent. My new duties are with my husband.'

'After so many years?' said Edith.

'He is not my husband,' said Clara. 'I suppose that he must take care of himself now, for he has no one left in the world.

You left him first, and now I am going to follow you in your perfidy. You have no right to accuse me, my dear Edith.'

'I do not,' she said; and after that remained silent, assisting her in dressing, and possibly thinking over her own wedding-day ten years before, and wondering whether Clara would ever be so unhappy as she had been.

There came a message from Mr. Wotherston, that he wished to see Miss Branscombe alone.

'Let him come up here,' said Clara to Edith. 'It is all over: let me know it all from his own mouth. I can bear it; do not fear for me; but it is hard.'

'Then you think,' said Edith, 'that when you had arranged to desert Lionel, your lover has deserted you?'

'Edith, you are talking fearful nonsense,'

said Clara, 'and you will find it out some day. Something has happened: I don't know what; but I knew that I was too happy; I knew that it could not be true.'

Edith went, and Wotherston entered hastily. She rose to meet him.

'Clara,' he said, hurriedly, 'I come to lay the future happiness of my life before you.'

'I am listening to you, James,' was all she said.

'You promised to marry me on condition that we should lead a very quiet life, and that you should not appear in London: we also arranged that we were to take Lionel to Italy with us. Now, my love, all these conditions shall be entirely fulfilled, if you choose; but I ask you to put them aside, and accept me on other terms.'

'And what are they?' she said.

'I *do* love politics so, Clara. I know that I am going to ask a heavy sacrifice; but I do ask you to stay here at Weston for the honeymoon, and give up going abroad.'

'I consent with great pleasure, my dear James,' she replied. 'May I ask why? and why it is you put such a stress on it? You have frightened me out of my wits. I thought that something dreadful had happened.'

'Clara,' said Wotherston, 'Langston is dead, and I am offered office.'

'Langston, Under Secretary of the Colonies?—and they have offered it to you?'

'Certainly. And will you, Clara, go to London in a fortnight, and take your place beside me? Will you return to the world which has treated you so cruelly, for my sake?'

'Old love, of course I will. Why do

you frighten me out of my life in this way?
But I must think: I don't see my way to it.'

'How?'

'I must have entirely new clothes,' said
Clara : ' my trousseau was made for a foreign
tour. I don't see how I can be ready in a
fortnight. But you will have to go to
London, and I will go with you : we can
manage it like that. Yes, that will be the
best way. *Don't say any more, James,*' she
whispered ; ' *walls have ears in this house.*'

With one lover's kiss he was gone, and
found Edith Branscombe remarkably near
the door. That fact of course he was too
hurried to notice.

The wedding between James Wotherston
and Clara was of a very quiet kind. The
bride and bridegroom, Lady Alice and Lady
Madeleine, Edith, and, for bestman to James
Wotherston, Struan, who happened to be on

a visit to Wotherston. He could not stay for the breakfast—he had business elsewhere; and he had no opportunity of speaking to Mrs. Lionel Branscombe. Father Wilson joined the party at the Grange, telling them that his vows prevented his entering a Protestant place of worship unless under the secret orders of his community.

There was a very pleasant breakfast. The Rector was agreeably surprised to find himself between Lady Alice and Lady Madeleine, and to discover that they knew as much about his poor as he did himself, which was a good deal. He also found himself consulted and looked up to by both of them, who seemed as though they were sitting at his feet and being instructed: this, with just a little brown sherry, made him regard the Grange and its Garden under a more mellow light, and he seemed ever

Q 2

afterwards, judging from his sermons, to think that there were worse people in the world than Evangelicals and Papists.

Old Mrs. Barton was not well, and the doctor was expected. They heard his brougham drive up to the door, and Lady Alice said to the servant, 'Show him in: it is a happy day, and he shall make one of us.' The servant departed.

'Let him rejoice with us,' said Lady Alice, 'for he seems to me not to get enough for shoe-leather, leave alone a brougham: and he has a good heart with him, and ain't afraid of the Board of Guardians. When little Martin Corry was sick of the fever, he ordered a bottle of port wine for him, and they sent him some of theirs, and he sent it back again saying that he wasn't going to have his patients poisoned. Good man, I'll go and see him in.'

She advanced towards the door, but before she reached it she—strong Irish woman as she was—actually reeled. For the door was thrown open, and the servant announced 'Mr. Branscombe.'

And there stood Arthur, with his hat idiotically on the back of his head and two parcels under his arms. He did not say anything, and did not look as if he was ever going to say anything more. Lady Alice rubbed her nose, returned to her seat, and went on with her breakfast, thereby giving the company to understand that she washed *her* hands of the whole business, and left it in the hands of Divine Providence. Arthur Branscombe, in trying to scratch his head, knocked his hat off, which the servant picked up and offered to him, whereupon Arthur Branscombe said to him, 'Not at all.'

Clara, with the swiftness of lightning,

saw what the poor fellow wanted there : she
hesitated but for one moment, and then she
went swiftly to him, and put her face in his,
spreading her white-clothed arms over his
black chest like a cross.

'Arthur! Arthur! you will forgive me,'
she said.

He turned his heavy, handsome face on
hers, and he said, 'Clara, can you forgive
me?'

And Father Wilson said to Lady Alice
Browne, 'There is more joy in heaven over
one sinner that repenteth than over ninety
and nine just men who need no repentance.'
And Lady Alice said nothing.

Wotherston rose and went to him. His
lameness had gone for a long time now,
and he looked every inch a bridegroom.
'Brother-in-law,' he said, 'this is very kind
of you. I thank you heartily.' And he

and Clara stood before him, both looking
as if they meant it, waiting to hear what he
was going to say.

That took a little time, but they knew
his habit. He first kissed Clara in a slow
and lumbering fashion; and Lady Alice
declares to this day that in his absence of
mind he was going to kiss James Wotherston
too, but was brought to his mind by drop-
ping one of his parcels: this one he picked
up and put in his hat, after which he put
his hat on, and assumed a confident air, as
if he had pegged several holes in a difficult
game at cribbage with his brother George.
He then proceeded slowly to the table and
sat down with his hat still upon his head,
and one of his parcels tucked under his arm.
Lady Alice Browne at once followed him,
took his hat off, and relieved him of
both of his parcels; then they all sat down

again, except Clara, who came and put her
arm about his neck : then he spoke.

  ' It is an uncommonly pleasant thing for
a fellow like me who has done no good in
the world, for a thing of this kind to happen.
For my poor neglected sister Clara, who has
gone through so much to marry a man like
Wotherston.   I heard about it from both
Wotherston and Struan, and I thought it
was only decent to step round with some
diamonds.   They have charged me fourteen
hundred for them, and they would have
cheated me; but you can't cheat my brother
George : he bought them ; he got his commission from me and his commission from
the jewellers, and so he has made a very
good thing out of it.   And what is so good
about my brother George is that he actually
brought them home all safe, which was

devilish gentlemanly, because any man but a perfect gentleman would have sold them, and gone off to California with the money. I have often said hard things about my brother George, but we must allow him to be a gentleman.'

Lady Alice rose and opened the two parcels, as Clara went and sat down. They contained jewel-cases; one had in it a torque, the other a bracelet. The gold-work was old-fashioned, and might have been worth fifty pounds, but six great blazing diamonds—two on the bracelet, four on the torque—perfectly accounted for the price which he said he had given for them. It was a splendid gift; and Clara bringing the things round to him asked him to fasten them on : he did so, and was rewarded with a kiss ; to which he only replied, ' My little

Clara!' and then asked Lady Madeleine if he might have some chicken, for he was hungry.

From his sudden appearance, and from what followed, our two good ladies had entirely forgotten the rites of hospitality. He was instantly supplied with everything he could wish for, and made a rapid but effectual breakfast.

'Your brother George, Arthur,' said Wotherston, ' or I should rather say *my* brother now, must be an excellent hand at a bargain.'

' He *is*,' said Arthur ; ' I have cause to know it. I would have given Clara some of the heirlooms, but in the first place I should have to give George one-third of the valued price, and in the second I did not like to give Clara anything which had not cost me money. I love my money, and I love her. And when you give things for love, you know——'

' I see,' said Wotherston.

' You were talking about my brother George just now, aunt.'

Lady Madeleine had been doing nothing of the kind. She said abruptly :

' If you had called me by that name oftener, Arthur Branscombe, we might have been better friends.'

' Ah, but I never liked to,' said Arthur. ' You were so high and refined that I was always ashamed of you,—I mean of myself.'

' Well, you will call me aunt in future, then,' said Lady Madeleine. ' It would not be ten thousand pounds' worth of diamonds which would make me say that, Arthur, but my steady growing good opinion of you. Last time you were here, we ignored our relationship. Let that cease. Now about your brother George.'

'Well, he is a very sober fellow. And sober fellows, I have remarked, generally like sweet things. I wish he might have some of this cream.'

'But you can't put it in your pocket,' said Lady Alice.

'No, but he is in the kitchen;— at least I told him to put the horse up at the inn, and go there.'

'Arthur,' said Lady Madeleine, 'this is the second time you have served us this trick.'

'I assure you,' said Arthur, 'that there is no trick about it, at least not to you. When we go abroad we always do a little business: I am the greatest breeder of carriage-horses in England, and George drives. Nobody knows him, and bless you he is worth all his money to me. Besides, we can trust one another, you know; our interests are identical; whereas I should be awfully cheated if I let one of my own grooms have anything to do with a bargain. The dealers try to buy him over, and cheat me, and so we get the best of them.'

The hopelessness of poor Arthur's morality in horse-dealing made that graceless person, Wotherston, laugh very loudly, and even Arthur relaxed into a smile. But Lady Alice had departed, and appeared at the door with George, who stood at the doorway smiling, and not one bit abashed.

The dapper handsome gambler of eight-and-thirty 'made up' splendidly as a fault-less groom of five-and-twenty: nothing could possibly have betrayed him except his perfect hands. If you had only put on him a red coat and a shirt collar, he would have been pronounced to be as well turned out as any dandy at Melton Mowbray.

'Well, my dear people,' he said, 'how are you all on this very joyful occasion? Lady Madeleine, I salute you; sister Clara, I congratulate you and your husband most heartily.'

But this would not do for either Clara or Wotherston. They treated him as they had treated Arthur, and when George felt his sister's arms round his neck he grew very much flushed, but kissed her heartily. Lady Alice saw that he would have liked to hide his eyes, but he could not.

'This is very kind of you, my girl, very kind of you,' he whispered; and no one heard him but Clara.

'You must come and sit down, George Branscombe,' said Lady Madeleine.

But this George flatly refused to do, in

his present dress; and as no urging would make him, they ceased to ask him: he insisted on taking his breakfast at the sideboard standing, but seemed to be very clumsy and slow about it. Clara saw by a gesture of his that he wanted her to come to him, and she went. They saw the pair with their backs towards them, her arm round his waist, just above his broad brown belt, and observed that he was apparently unbuttoning his coat: then they looked no more. In a few moments Clara returned to the table with something clasped tightly in her right hand.

Well, the poor devil had given her his watch, a beautiful little Breguet, taken in payment most probably for some gambling transaction; it was all he had to give, and he gave it to her. In her eyes, at all events, it was more precious than Arthur's diamonds.

They separated. But none had noticed that Edith had disappeared from the first: none knew that she was sobbing upon the bed, and saying to herself, wildly, ' Oh, why did I ever leave the convent! Let me go back!—let me go back! IIis brothers!'

CHAPTER XVII.

GEORGE HANGS UP HIS WHIP.

GEORGE, one morning very soon after their return from their trip to Clara's wedding, which trip they had prolonged for business, was in the stable yard at his usual hour of half-past six in summer (he was never later than half-past seven in winter). He was smartly dressed in breeches and shoes, from which the grooms and helpers judged that they were to see some horsemanship,—for when any peculiarly dangerous thing had to be done George always left his boots at home and rode in stockings and shoes. We must do him the credit to say that he did not look like the comic Irishman in this gear, but like a perfect gentleman. Some men can wear anything, and George was one.

He attended to everything and every-body, but swore at nothing, to everybody's great surprise. Lastly, he ordered out a young horse, and ordered him to be har-nessed to a very old brougham which was kept by Arthur, as the Admiralty keeps the 'Oberon,' for torpedo and gunnery expe-riments. It had been kicked to pieces very often, but had been tinkered up again in a marvellous manner: it really looked like a real brougham still (it was afterwards sold, and is now a successful station fly).

The young horse which was now har-nessed to this brougham was a considerable mystery to both Arthur and George. The beast looked worth 200*l.*, but George had

got him for thirty-five; there was something
the matter with him, and Arthur had fra-
ternally asked George to find out what it
was for him.

As George was sitting on his brother's
bed the night before, Arthur had said, 'We
can't lose, and yet I should like to know
about him, because I don't want another
action on warranty. I don't think it's the
collar; I think it is the saddle. If he does
go right in the collar, put the saddle on
him and make Jacob try him.'

'But if he is all right in harness we can
sell him.'

'To *drive*, but if we can't say " ride and
drive," it's ten pound off his price. If he is
right with the collar alone, we can sell him
to the Doctor.'

Arthur did not mean Cross, but the
Parish Doctor.

'But he wants to ride sometimes,' said George.

'Well, if we can sell him the horse as a carriage horse, and never mention the riding, he can't come on me for damages if he tries to ride the horse and breaks his neck.'

'Well, I will see what can be done to-morrow morning,' said George; and so we find the young horse saddled to the 'Oberon' brougham with kicking-strap, and also a gag; for although George was not cruel to horses—he was too good a horseman for that —yet, as he put it, he liked to be on the safe side.

George fancied that he very soon found out what was the matter with him,—the horse was almost preternaturally slow, and so sluggish in temper, that even when George lost his own over the *vis inertiæ* of the brute, and flogged it severely, only a funereal trot could be got out of it, and George was afraid that it would not even do for the Doctor.

So he told them to put the saddle on it, and Jacob was preparing to mount, but George would not let him,—there was something worse than he knew of about the horse, and it was not fair to have the young man knocked about any more; he thought that he would speak to Arthur about it, for Jacob, the pluckiest of all the grooms, used generally to volunteer for any dangerous work, and have his services promptly accepted by Arthur. George therefore thought it only fair to incur this unknown danger himself.

He was no sooner mounted than he found out what it was; before he had time to think of anything, before his reins were well gathered together, the horse had his head down nearly between his knees, and was 'bucking' all over the yard. George sat splendidly, laughing at the sudden discovery of the mysterious vice, though rather cross at he and Arthur having been led into the purchase of a horse which was practically worth not five pounds. He was thinking of slipping quietly off, when the brute put one of his feet on an iron drain at one side of the yard and came heavily down with him, throwing him on the bricks with great violence on his right side, which was undefended, as his arm was raised preparing to cut the horse with his whip to see what that would do. It was a very heavy fall, and the men ran up, but George was on his legs before the horse, looking rather pale, and rubbing the dust off his coat with his pocket-handkerchief.

'There's thirty pounds of Arthur's money

gone,' he said aloud. ' The brute is not worth
a fiver.'

When the horse was got to his legs, it
was found that he was worth less, for he had
broken one of them. George went up to
tell his brother. He explained what had
happened to the horse.

' Beast,' said Arthur. ' Go and tell them
to shoot the poor devil at once. Was Jacob
hurt, brother ? '

' I was riding him, and I got a thundering
cropper on my right side, but I don't think
I am hurt.'

' But why did you not put Jacob on him?'
said Arthur. ' Are you sure you are not
hurt ? '

' I have got a bruise, that's all,' said
George. ' I didn't think it fair on Jacob to
put him up; he was emptied off only last
week.'

'It was kind of you,' said Arthur, 'but I wish you would take more care of yourself. Come and eat your breakfast.'

But George could not do that very well; he tried, but it was a failure; he said that he was afraid he had had a very bad shaking. Arthur made him eat a piece of bread and take some cordial, but he said that he must lie down a little; he went on to a sofa and lay on his left side; Arthur coming up, opened his shirt and gently felt his side, and when he touched one place George gave a low moan.

Arthur left him without a word, but ordered his brougham instantly, and after an hour returned in the company of a grave, pleasant-looking man.

This was the Doctor whom he was going to cheat into buying his horse that morning. He would have given him one for a present now. He had felt enough on George's side to tell him, as an anatomist, there was something very wrong.

When they approached George he was quiet, but breathing rather heavily: the Doctor, upon saluting George and feeling his pulse, procured a large pair of scissors from the housekeeper, and proceeded methodically to cut George's clothes off his back. Arthur expected that George would have protested; but George said, 'You *must* do that. I couldn't take them off;' and added mournfully, 'I paid cash for that coat because the fellow would not let me have tick. I wish he had now.'

When George's clothes were removed, his brother, who had not seen him stripped for years, noticed that he had A. C., a heart, and on the other side of it G. B., tattooed on his left breast. Many hours afterwards, after

long reflection, Arthur came to the conclusion
that George had been in love with somebody
else some time or another. He was pro-
foundly astonished. 'It must have been a
precious long time ago,' he said to himself
at last.

Things were very bad, as Arthur had
suspected from the first. A rib was broken,
which was certainly pressing on the lung, if
not penetrating it. It was obvious that with
the greatest care and good fortune George
Branscombe's earthly career was run; and,
as the Doctor remarked to himself, he was
certainly not fit for a heavenly one.

Arthur's grief was unbounded: he took
the Doctor into his confidence. 'You see,
Doctor, I haven't done my duty by him, any
more than I did by my sister Clara; and I
have lost—as a friend—the only friend I
ever made. But since Mr. Struan came here,

do you see, he has pointed out to me, and I think to George, how much better we could get on together if we yielded more. And I thought that I should have made a friend of him, and now he is going to die. I shall be all alone, with the memory of my sins for company, now. I wish it was I instead of he.'

The grooms with whom George had so often quarrelled came in and carried the couch on which George lay up the grand staircase to Arthur's room; and when they laid him down at the foot of his brother's bed he thanked them humbly and asked them to forgive him.

END OF THE SECOND VOLUME.

Spottiswoode & Co., Printers, New-street Square, London.